GHOST
STORIES
of
WISCONSIN

GHOST STORIES
of
WISCONSIN

A.S. Mott

Lone Pine Publishing International

The Publisher: Lone Pine Publishing International
Distributed by Lone Pine Publishing
1808 B Street NW, Suite 140
Auburn, WA 98001
USA

Websites: www.lonepinepublishing.com
www.ghostbooks.net

National Library of Canada Cataloguing in Publication Data

Mott, A. S. (Allan S.), 1975-
   Ghost stories of Wisconsin / A.S. Mott.

   ISBN-13: 978-976-8200-21-1
   ISBN-10: 976-8200-21-9

   1. Ghosts--Wisconsin.   2. Legends--Wisconsin.   I. Title.

GR110.W5M68 2006   398.209775'05   C2006-903542-3

The stories, folklore and legends in this book are based on the author's collection of sources including individuals whose experiences have led them to believe they have encountered phenomena of some kind or another. They are meant to entertain, and neither the publisher nor the author claims these stories represent fact.

PC: P5

To Mr. Lombardi

Who once said,
"If you'll not settle for anything less than your best,
you will be amazed at what
you can accomplish in your lives."
And who was right when he said it.

Contents

Acknowledgments

It takes more than one man typing like a demon at his computer keyboard to create a book like this—not much more, but more nonetheless. It is because of this golden truth that I must take the time to thank those who aided me in transforming a terrifying expanse of blank screen into the work you hold in your hands. Without them you would be reading something else right now.

First I must thank my friends, those patient souls who have chosen to go on enduring the quirks of my personality for the sake of the rare moment when I prove amusing. Dan Asfar was always ready to listen from across the ocean as I bored him with the petty details of my working travails. Michelle Green gave me constant comfort and support in her emails and comments on my blog. My editor, Carol Woo, was only too happy to let me join her as she got her necessary coffee fix. And how could I forget my heroes in the cool part of the office—Shelley, Carmen, Chris, Sal, Ken, Faye, Bridget and Jennifer—who were always willing to pretend that my jokes weren't annoying them and that I wasn't interrupting the important work they were doing.

Sadly, writing this book kept me away from my family, but I don't think they minded that much. Still, I thank them for their patience and for admitting they were related to me when people noticed that they shared a last name with "the guy who wrote those books."

I also have to thank Sheila Quinlan for making me look smarter than I am through her editing and Willa Kung for making my manuscript look remarkably book-like.

And most of all I have to thank you, my readers. There may not be a lot of you out there, but I have always believed that quality is better than quantity.

Introduction

I have a theory.

It goes like this. The first story ever told was an adventure story—maybe it was the thrilling tale of a successful hunt or an intense recounting of a daring escape from a dangerous predator. The second story ever told was a joke—most likely in the form of a funny tale about a much less successful hunt or about the time Bob the caveman successfully fooled everyone into thinking he was a woman. The third story ever told was a romance—a moving drama about how a young cavewoman fell in love with the caveman of her dreams when he came back from the hunt with a delicious animal she had never tasted before.

And then came the fourth story. It—I would wager you everything I own (which admittedly would make for something of a sucker's bet)—was a ghost story. It was, no doubt, a sad, scary thriller about a man who did not come back from the hunt and who returned in a form that was nothing like the one he left behind.

What I'm suggesting is that stories like the ones found in this book go back a long way. We're talking thousands of years before mankind even figured out a way to write them down. Yet despite their having been around for all that time, we have yet to become tired of them. How can this be?

I think it is because we all enjoy imagining—if not actually believing in—a world where death is not the end. We also like to think it is possible to know a little about what awaits us after the Reaper has knocked on our door and found a way inside the house after we rudely refused to let him in.

But that is not the only reason we enjoy a good ghost story. I know, from having had the experience of reading from my books to people between the ages of 8 and 80, that different people like these stories for different reasons. My most enthusiastic audiences, for example, are invariably young kids who have not yet had to confront the idea that their lives are not eternal. These second and third graders couldn't care less about the mysteries of the afterlife—they're too busy enjoying the jumps and scares that come from walking down the spooky side of the street. Older folks, on the other hand, are less interested in being scared than they are in exploring the interesting ideas these stories cause to percolate inside their minds.

The enduring power of the ghost story is made most clear by how strong it remains today in an age where mankind's ability to entertain itself has reached a level that would most probably make a caveman's head explode if he were confronted by it. Although we no longer have to spend our nights telling tales about the hunt around a roaring fire, we still want to hear the same kind of stories we have been hearing since we started sorting out this whole language situation.

But then I really don't have to explain this to you, do I? I mean, if you're reading this then you know exactly how good it feels to immerse yourself in the world of paranormal prose and are likely waiting me for to wrap this whole introduction up so you can get to the good bits you paid to read. Well, I won't keep you any longer. Here are a whole bunch of supernatural tales from the great state of Wisconsin. I hope you enjoy them.

1
Ghosts of the Cursed and Murdered

Fairlawn

Horace wasn't a big fan of museums, which was odd considering how much time he spent in them. He worked as a traveling rep for a marketing firm that specialized in helping small towns take in lucrative tourist income by learning how to accentuate and promote their unique charms. Unfortunately for him, most of those unique charms weren't that unique, and many of the towns he traveled to were the type of places a person was more likely to become stuck in by accident rather than visit by design. And each one of those places had a museum.

Often that was all they had, beyond the requisite fast-food outlet and box department store. True, some of these museums were better than others, but most of them were depressingly the same. There was only so much old furniture and period clothing a normal person could see in one lifetime before their appeal no longer satisfied the soul. Horace had reached that point years ago.

It was for that reason that he took no pleasure in what he saw inside Superior's Fairlawn. It was a beautiful Victorian house built in the exquisite Queen Anne style, but its charms had no effect on him whatsoever. He had been in several other beautiful Victorian mansions that simply oozed Queen Anne-ness, and though this was easily one of the nicer ones, it still had little to offer that excited him.

As Horace took the tour and learned the building's history, he was once again incapable of feeling anything other than blasé. The home had been built by Superior's first mayor, a lumber baron named Martin Pattison, who started construction on the $150,000 mansion in 1889 and completed it two years later. He lived there with his wife, Grace, and their six children. Two years after his death in 1918, his family moved to California and donated the property to the Superior Children's Home and Refuge Association, which used it as an orphanage. It served in that capacity for 42 years, until 1962 when the town bought it for $12,500 and turned it into the museum it is today. Since that time, a $1.6 million restoration project has brought the old building back to its former glory.

To the handful of tourists that surrounded Horace, this was all fascinating stuff, but he thought it was the snooze of all time. It might have been interesting if he hadn't heard the same story with different names in dozens of other towns around the country.

The tour soon ended, and he and the other visitors were now free to walk around the building at their leisure. While the others enjoyed the displays the museum had set up around the building, as well as the art that could be found almost everywhere, Horace had only one place he wanted to be, but he was having difficulty finding it. His desire to visit this part of the building grew more intense with each passing minute, and his body became visibly agitated as it kept being denied.

Finally a museum employee who—unlike the woman who had given the tour—was dressed in period maid's clothing noticed his distress and came up to him. "Can I help you, sir?" she asked him. She spoke with a heavy Scandinavian accent, which suggested that she was still fairly new to the country (or that she was just a good actress who was a stickler for period detail).

"I can't find the men's washroom," Horace informed her, too anxious to notice the oddly damp chill that came upon the air.

"It is a bit out of the way," the woman admitted. "Follow me and I'll show you where it is."

"Thanks," he said with genuine gratitude.

"It's a pleasure," she smiled at him. She was really rather pretty. "Right this way," she said as she started walking toward the washroom.

It turned out that Horace had actually walked past the men's room several times in his search for it, but he was too grateful to have finally found it to be embarrassed, and he rushed inside. When he came back out, the helpful woman in the period costume was gone.

Horace was ready to leave the museum, but before he did he saw the woman who had given the tour he had taken. Seeing her, he couldn't help but wonder why she too wasn't dressed in a period maid's uniform, like the other woman had been. He decided to ask her.

The woman appeared to be very surprised to hear the question. "You saw a woman in a maid's uniform?" she asked, sounding as if he was trying to pull a prank on her.

"Yeah, she showed me where the men's washroom was."

"What did she sound like?"

"Pardon me?"

"Did she have some kind of accent?"

"Oh, yeah, she sounded like a Swedish stewardess in a bad 60s sitcom."

"Sir," said the tour guide, "I don't want to scare you, but I think you just met Ingrid, Fairlawn's own personal ghost."

"What?"

"You're not the first person to have met her. She's very friendly."

"She was a ghost?"

"That's right."

Horace was impressed. He hadn't seen one of those before.

*   *   *

Like many wealthy families of the period, the Pattisons used indentured servitude as a means to keep their large household properly staffed. This practice saw a wealthy person agree to pay for an immigrant's passage to America in exchange for that person's services for a specified period of time. It wasn't a perfect system, but for many poor people it represented their best—and only—chance to start a life in the land of opportunity.

Those folks who struck such a deal with Martin Pattison, who had the kind of generous soul that is seldom found in men of his wealth and stature, found themselves extremely lucky. In other houses, these men and women would have been treated as little more than legal slaves, but in Fairlawn they were treated as respected members of the family. Because of this treatment, it wasn't uncommon for some servants to stay on and continue working for the family long after they had paid off their original debt.

One grateful servant was a Swedish girl named Ingrid, who considered the time she spent working as a maid for the Pattisons the happiest years of her life. Her life back home had been very hard. Her mother had died young and had left her with a drunken father whose quick temper often resulted in violent beatings for his daughter. Ingrid had no education, could not read or write and spoke no English. She agreed to travel across the ocean to work for a family who lived in a place she had never heard of before because as frightening as it seemed, it still had to be better than where she was.

Her gamble paid off. She took to English like she had always known it somewhere in the back of her mind, and one of the Pattison daughters made it her mission to cure Ingrid of her illiteracy. For the first time in her life, Ingrid felt as though she had found a place where she belonged, so it made sense that when her period of indebted service was over, she was very reluctant to leave. She probably wouldn't have if she hadn't met Reggie.

Reggie was the handsome son of a family that was acquainted with the Pattisons. Most guests took no notice of the help, but Reggie had been immediately struck by Ingrid's sweet, blond beauty. As a pretty servant girl, she often had to deal with the unwanted advances of wealthy men who considered anyone in a maid's uniform fair game for the taking. Ingrid had developed a firm, but polite, way to rebuff these unwanted overtures.

But it was different when Reggie announced his affection for her. For one thing, he didn't do it by pulling her into a hidden spot and talking to her in a hushed tone so no one else could hear—he instead declared his feelings in front of everyone, including his own parents, who were horrified by his lack of discretion.

He didn't care. Reggie was a rebel, and if he wanted to fall in love with a servant girl, then he wasn't going to hide it. Ingrid, for her part, did her best not to encourage his behavior, but then one day Mr. Pattison summoned her to his office so he could talk with her.

Ingrid had talked with Mr. Pattison many times during the course of her employment, but this was the first time he had ever requested to meet with her in this manner. She was very nervous as she walked into the room and saw him sitting behind his desk, reading the local newspaper.

"Ah, Ingrid," he smiled at her, "please come in and sit down."

"Thank you, Mr. Pattison," she said respectfully as she sat down in the chair in front of his desk.

"Why do look so nervous, my dear?" asked her employer.

"I'm not sure, Mr. Pattison," she admitted.

"Well, stop it," he said gently, but firmly. "It makes me feel sinister."

"I'm sorry, sir," she apologized as she attempted to adopt a more relaxed appearance.

"Now, do you know why I wanted to talk to you?"

"Is it about Mr. Harris, sir?"

"Yes it is," Mr. Pattison answered with a nod. "It's very clear to everyone that he holds you in high regard."

"Does he, sir?"

"Don't pretend to be so innocent, Ingrid," he said. "It is obvious that he is very much taken with you."

"I suppose you're right, sir," she admitted, "but I've tried hard not to encourage him."

"Ay, now that's why I brought you in here. I wanted to let you know that—if you happen to feel the same way about him that he does for you—I see no earthly reason for you not to let him know it."

"But, sir," she said, surprised by what he had just said to her, "his parents would not approve."

"I find the Harrises to be very tiring people, Ingrid," he admitted. "They're snobs, and I have no use for people with such outdated attitudes. This country isn't some European monarchy with a rigid class system. It's America, where a person's current station in life should never be considered a barrier to their future! If Reginald Harris' intentions are noble and he truly thinks of you as someone he wants in his life, then I shall not get in the way of that. If, on the other hand, it becomes apparent that all he wants is to take your virtue and then marry someone else, then I would also have no problem with you slapping him in the face. Either way, I wanted it to be clear that whatever you choose to do in this matter, I will support you."

"Thank you, sir," she said as a few stray tears started misting her eyes.

"Now, now," he said, "let's have none of that. You can go back to work now."

"Yes, sir," she said as she stood up and started walking out of the room. She made it to the door, but then she felt compelled to stop and say one last thing. "You're a good man, Mr. Pattison," she told her employer.

"Thank you, Ingrid," he smiled back at her.

With her employer's blessing, Ingrid let Reggie know that she reciprocated his feelings and would be happy to get to know him better outside of Fairlawn. As he courted her, his parents threatened to cut him off financially, telling him that they would not pay to see him married to a foreign servant girl. Never one to take well to any kind of threat, Reggie reacted to their ultimatum by proposing to Ingrid that very day. She said yes, and they were married a month later. His parents did not attend the wedding and made good on their threat by cutting off his access to any of the family fortune. Mr. Pattison paid for the wedding, which was held at Fairlawn. That fairy-tale day would be last day she would spend there while she was still alive.

Despite being cut off financially, Reggie had made enough social connections during his years at private school to find work that kept the two of them financially comfortable—at least, for a time. Although they were far from poor, Reggie's earnings were not enough to keep him within the circle of people he had grown up with. They were all extremely wealthy and could afford to hold lavish parties and indulge in frequent trips overseas. In contrast, Reggie and his wife lived, at best, a life that was tediously middle class. Over time, Reggie came to resent the limitations his marriage had forced upon his life. By their fifth anniversary, his love for the sweet Swedish maid he had married had transformed into something dark and ugly.

Ingrid, for her part, had no idea what she could have possibly done to earn her husband's enmity. As far as she was concerned, their situation couldn't be more perfect. Having been raised in dire poverty, the experience of middle-class life was, for her, filled with countless luxuries she never dreamed she would ever enjoy. She couldn't understand why they were not good enough for Reggie, nor could she comprehend the sacrifice he felt he had made to marry her.

At first, Reggie's anger toward her showed itself in frequent insults and criticisms regarding her accent, manners and lack of education. He often belittled her in front of others and made her feel stupid whenever a conversation turned to subjects she knew nothing about, like art, history or politics. In time, his anger grew into a rage that was very often physical in nature. He became extremely unpredictable and could fly into a destructive fury without a second's notice, with most of it invariably landing upon Ingrid, whose past had already taught her how to hide bruises and other injuries from the outside world.

But the moment fate truly turned against her was when Reggie received a letter from his mother. This was the first contact he'd had with his family since before the wedding. In it, his mother told him that his father was dying and was prepared to forgive Reggie's marriage to the maid—if the marriage no longer existed before he died.

Knowing that he had no legal cause for divorce, nor the time to fake any, Reggie saw only one way to ensure that his marriage to Ingrid was over before his ailing father was dead. Claiming he had to travel out of town on business, he left her alone in their home. As she slept, he broke into the house as if he were a burglar. He then crept to their bedroom and wrapped his bare hands around her neck. She awoke as he tightened his grip, but no matter how much she struggled and fought against him, she could not get him to let go. It took a very long time for her to die, but Reggie was very determined and did not give up until he was sure that she was gone.

It turned out, though, that his crime was for naught. His father died that same night and his will went unchanged—Reggie did not receive a penny of the fortune. The police were easily able to connect him to his wife's murder, and not long after it he was arrested. He was sentenced to death for his crime, but before his execution could be carried out he was killed by an illness he had contracted from another prisoner.

And that was how the fairy tale ended.

*   *   *

Fairlawn had already been transformed into an orphanage by the time Ingrid was killed by her husband. That was why her spirit seemed so out of place when it first appeared in the converted mansion. Two boys were the first to spot her, and they asked her why she was wearing such an odd uniform. She answered them by insisting that there was nothing odd about what she was wearing because it was what she worked in every day. Before they could question her any further, she vanished.

When her spirit was finally identified, it became common wisdom that she haunted the mansion while dressed in her maid's uniform simply because that represented the one time in her life when she was truly happy. Unlike so many other ghosts who focus only on their pain and misery, Ingrid's spirit ignored the ugliness she faced in life and instead remained on Earth to recreate the brief period in which she felt truly blessed.

Although she was only seen occasionally during the years the mansion served as an orphanage, she appeared much more frequently once it was turned into a museum. It makes sense when you consider that this transition meant that the house she adored was remade in the image she remembered it.

Since then many other tourists—most of whom are not as blasé as Horace—have told of being helped by the pretty blond woman in the period dress who spoke with the

Scandinavian accent. And it goes without saying that all of them treasured their visit to the museum much more than they normally would have once they learned that they saw something even more special than antique furniture in a beautiful Victorian setting—they saw a truly happy spirit.

A Sad Tale of Fire and Ice

Although he had never been the type of person to say too much about anything, Evan Lewis could, if he had ever been asked, expound for hours on the potential disparities between the body and the mind. It was a subject in which he had become an expert, not through study, but through experience, starting from the moment all of his peers noticed that he was bigger and stronger than any of them could ever hope to be.

There had never been a moment in Evan's life in which he knew what it was like to be small. By the age of seven, he was as tall as his mother; by the age of nine, he had surpassed the height of his father. By the time he turned 13, he stood six feet and five inches tall, and that was where he stayed for the rest of his life. He never had the opportunity to be weighed on a scale, but if he had, he likely would have tipped the machine around 275 pounds. Even though he was still a young boy in his heart and mind, he was—to the rest of the world—a large, intimidating man.

Evan found his size to be both a blessing and a curse. The blessing was that he had the strength necessary to defend himself whenever he got into a fight, and the curse was that he found himself using that strength far more often than anyone would ever want to. He was a shy, quiet boy, and though it was not within his nature to pick fights, they had a way of finding him no matter how hard he tried to avoid them.

To some of the older kids in Ridgeway, Evan's size was not as intimidating as it was a challenge to be conquered. Older boys would seek out Evan and confront him so they could prove to their friends how tough they were. No one ever stopped to consider that it didn't require a lot of courage to pick a fight with a much younger boy. Still few, if any, of his challengers ever walked away from the fight with anything but a bruised ego and a host of physical injuries to match.

Because Evan had an unfortunate tendency to always come out on top of these encounters, he was always the one who was punished for them afterward. No matter how hard he protested that he had not been the one to start a fight, he could not deny that he had been the one to finish it. The result was that he earned a reputation around town for being a bully and was eventually expelled from school.

Many people have found themselves cursed with an undeserved reputation. In Evan's case, it was only a matter of time before he realized that as long as people believed he was a bully and treated him as such, he might as well accept the role and enjoy the benefits that came with it.

*   *   *

Just a few miles from Ridgeway stood a crossroads connecting roads throughout the state. These roads brought many travelers into town, most of whom stopped to rest or eat, and although many of these travelers were good people who meant no harm to anyone, some were not. Few of these scoundrels who came into town ever stayed for longer than a day—that was more than enough time to rob a fellow traveler in a crooked card game or by putting a knife to some hapless fellow's throat.

Still, as quickly as these black-hearted men came and went through Ridgeway, they did have a place they could stay. There was a tavern that no decent person would consider entering if they wished their mind, body and wallet to remain unharmed. It was called McKillip's Saloon, and at the age of 16, Evan was hired to be its bouncer.

Back then it was rare for a local saloon to hire someone to specifically enforce the peace and remove anyone who disturbed it, but at McKillip's it was a full-time job that seldom ever allowed the person who held the position to take a break. It was also a position that needed to be filled quite often, as most of the men who took the job lasted barely a week before they quit or were too seriously injured to continue working. Evan's most immediate predecessor had only been there two days before his right ear had been sliced off by a patron who had had one drink too many.

The job was so dangerous that it had become virtually impossible for Leo McKillip, the saloon's owner, to find anyone who was willing to take it. That was why he decided to seek out Ridgeway's famous young bully and attempt to convince him that he could earn some good money intimidating some of the most violent and frightening men in the entire state.

At the time, Evan was helping his father at the family butcher shop, learning the trade and dealing with customers. He was miserable. He hated cutting meat, and he hated the way people looked at him suspiciously whenever he served them. He could tell that most of them assumed he was cheating them by overweighing their purchases, but none of them was brave enough to call him on it. After a while he became so infuriated that he actually did start overweighing the meat and made some money pocketing the difference. If everyone was going to assume he was a crook anyway, then there was no point in being honest. Luckily for his dad, theirs was the only butcher shop in town, which meant that Evan's thievery did not affect business. Still, the senior Lewis was concerned that having Evan work at the store for much longer might start to drive away customers.

But that didn't mean he was happy when Leo McKillip came into the store and offered Evan the job of bouncer at the saloon—he was well aware of the establishment's reputation, and he did not want his son working in such a place. He ordered Evan not to take the job, but McKillip was offering four times as much money as Evan made at the butcher shop (including the cash he was cheating out of customers). McKillip also offered the chance to do something that did not involve any kind of animal carcass (with the exception of the occasional human being).

It was a deal Evan could not refuse.

*   *   *

Evan had never stepped foot inside of that saloon or any other, so he was not at all prepared for what he found.

From the outside, the saloon looked almost like a church that had been taken deep down into the Earth and scorched in the fires of hell, and that wasn't too far from the truth. The building had once been a church. Long abandoned and gone to seed, the place was acquired by McKillip in 1836 in a hand of poker he had won thanks to one of the dozen aces he habitually tucked into his left boot.

McKillip had decided to use this recent windfall to turn the old church into a saloon. His aim was for something that could usually only be found in towns with interesting names like Dead Man's Hollow and Reaper's Bastion (in other words, places not quite as classy or upscale as Deadwood and Tombstone). He spent some money tearing out the building's interior and adding a large fireplace, just like the one in that place in Iowa where he lost his pinky finger to pay off a bar bet. As for the exterior, it didn't make sense to improve it too much; his regular clientele wouldn't appreciate the effort, and it would probably encourage the wrong element (i.e., honest folks) to pop their heads in for a visit. So, apart from slapping on a coat of the same cheap red paint that people used for barns, he left the outside of the building alone.

Evan was so spooked by the building's façade that it took him a second to get the courage up to walk through its front door. Once he did, he wanted—almost instantly—to turn right back around and walk out.

For all of his life Evan had never understood why people found him so frightening and intimidating, but now that he was standing in a room full of dangerous, violent-looking men, he got it. Although none of the other men in the saloon were as big as he was, they all possessed an identical dark aura of anger, apathy and avarice, and each one was obviously capable of killing someone in an instant and never once feeling any guilt for having done it.

And as Evan stood in the doorway, the heads of all of these terrible souls turned toward him and studied him with the practiced, emotionless gaze of those who made their living taking advantage of the fears of other men. Evan understood immediately that it was this moment that would determine whether he kept this job or started running all the way back home. If he showed them the slightest indication of the frightened boy he truly was under all of the muscle and bone, they would eat him alive; but if he proved to them that he was not someone to trifle with, there was a chance he might make it.

He stole a glance around the room and searched for the second biggest man in the saloon, the biggest being himself. He found who he was looking for sitting at a table beside the large fireplace. With a frown, he clenched his fists and started walking over to the table. As he walked he looked over to McKillip, who was standing behind the bar serving drinks. His boss understood what Evan was doing and approved it with a smile and a wink.

Before the other man could stand up, Evan punched him in the jaw as hard as he could. The man collapsed to the ground with a loud thud, trying to protest the randomness of Evan's assault, but he couldn't because the powerful punch had broken his jaw. Evan then bent over and attempted to pick up the man, who was very heavy and not particularly happy about having just been knocked to the floor for no reason, but before the wounded fellow could retaliate, Evan punched him again and knocked him unconscious. The man no longer presented a struggle, and Evan grunted as he lifted the unlucky patron off of the floor and carried him to the saloon's door. Once there, he threw the man through the doorway like he was a sack of potatoes.

During this time, not one of the other patrons moved or made a sound. When Evan turned back toward them, they all returned to what they had been doing before he had walked inside.

Evan's hand hurt worse than it ever had before, but he betrayed no pain as he walked to the bar and presented himself to his new employer.

"Good job, kid," McKillip congratulated him. "That was really smart thinking. Now that these scoundrels know what you can do to them, they'll all think twice before giving you any trouble. Shame about what you did to my brother, though."

"That was your brother?" Evan couldn't stop himself from exclaiming.

"Don't worry about it," said McKillip. "He owes me 10 dollars, so he'll probably just assume I told you to do that to him to remind him, which I probably would have done anyway. Good news is I can probably expect him to pay me back right away, or he'll leave town and never come back. Either way I'm a happy man."

"Who's the killer?" came a woman's voice from behind Evan's back.

Evan turned around and saw a small woman dressed in an outfit that made him blush. Looking at her he could imagine a time—10 or 15 years ago—when she might have been pretty, especially if she had possessed all of her teeth back then.

"This is Evan, our new bouncer," McKillip informed the woman. "Evan, this is Lucy."

Lucy introduced him to the less anti-social regulars. Along the way he got a sense of the saloon's layout, including the back rooms where Lucy's "girls" did the majority of their "work." Eventually he was able to pry himself loose from Lucy's grasp and return to the bar, where Leo already had a job for him.

"I'm afraid this going to be your first true test, my boy," McKillip told him with a look that made it clear he wasn't joking. "Desmond Porter just came in, even though last week I banned him from this establishment for the rest of his life."

"What did he do?" asked Evan, trying to conjure up an idea of something so horrible it would result in a permanent exile from even this place.

"He spat tobacco juice all over my floor instead of into a spittoon. It's the one offence I just can't forgive. You're going to have to tell him to leave or else all of these other animals are going to think I've gone soft, and before you can blink we'll be up to our knees in that brown goop."

"Which one is he?"

"He's that unpleasant-looking fella standing over there," answered McKillip, pointing over to the scariest-looking human being Evan had ever seen.

"*Him*?" gulped Evan.

"He's not as tough as he looks," insisted McKillip, though Evan could tell he was lying. "Just don't look him in the eye or touch him in an area where he's ticklish and you'll be fine."

"Ticklish?"

"Trust me."

Evan took another look at his quarry, wondering for a moment how he had gotten himself into this situation, and then he sighed and went to work. As he walked over to Porter he saw the man spit a big wad of chewing tobacco onto the floor. Leo was right—things would get very unpleasant if everyone started aping this crude behavior.

"Excuse me," Evan spoke to the back of Porter's head in his deepest, most masculine voice, "but I'm going to have to ask you to leave." He waited for the man to turn around, which he did very slowly and deliberately. It took all of Evan's resolve not to flinch when he discovered that not everyone who loses an eye in a knife fight bothers to cover up the resulting hole with an eye patch.

"And who, pray tell, is doing the asking?" sneered Porter.

"I am," said Evan, not backing down. "You have to the count of five, and then I get physical."

"You can count that high, then? I never would have guessed."

"One."

"I wonder where McKillip picked you up—it's not like there are any zoos around these parts."

"Two."

"Did he tell you that the last guy he sent over to ask me to leave left behind a widow and two young kids?"

"Three."

"I shoved a knife into his navel and cut all the way up to his Adam's Apple. Lucky for him it was a sharp knife."

"Four."

"You don't scare easy, I'll give you that."

"Fi—"

Before Evan could finish Porter pulled out a large knife and plunged it toward him, but Evan's reflexes were much quicker than anyone could have expected, and he was able to grab Porter's hand and stop the knife before it went into his chest. He squeezed Porter's wrist with all of his might until it broke with a loud, sickening snap. The knife dropped to the ground and an enraged Porter tried to swing at Evan with his undamaged arm, but the boy was too quick for him and was able block the punch without any trouble at all. Evan then punched Porter as hard as he could in the nose, breaking it with a squish. Porter screamed as blood poured down his face, but his screaming stopped when Evan hit him again and knocked him unconscious.

His opponent vanquished, Evan lifted the man's body from the ground and heaved it out of the saloon's front door. When he turned around, he could see that this time he had really made an impression on the regulars. It was one thing to sucker punch someone who wasn't expecting it, but it was quite another to face Desmond Porter and come out without even a scratch.

Evan, who had never drank a drop of alcohol before that night, quickly got drunk as everyone in the bar tried to get on his good side by buying him a drink.

*   *   *

Within a week, word had spread across the entire state that at Ridgeway's McKillip's Saloon there was a bouncer who was not to be trifled with. As those who had been in the bar on Evan's first night repeated the story of how quickly and easily he had defeated "Empty Eye" Porter, his reputation as a man to be feared grew greater each day.

As his legend grew, his job became easier and easier. Soon whole weeks would fly by without his having to use his fists, as he could settle nearly every situation merely by looking over at those who were causing it. Rather than face his wrath, nearly everyone thought better of what they were doing and quickly left the bar without suffering any needless injury.

Somehow, without really knowing how he had done it, Evan had done the impossible and turned the most dangerous bar in Ridgeway into a place that was nearly safe enough to hold a tea party, albeit one surrounded by extremely unsavory characters.

Some of the saloon's regulars grumbled that this change in atmosphere made the place a lot less fun to drink in. However, most agreed that it was nice to be able to sit down and drink without having to worry that someone was going to throw a knife into your back.

There was only one person who was truly unhappy with the new status quo, and that was the man who had made the legend of Evan Lewis possible. Desmond Porter seethed with rage as his own reputation took a painful beating; the constant retellings of his encounter with the saloon's bouncer made him look more and more foolish and pathetic with each passing day. He knew that he would have to kill Evan Lewis if he were ever to get back his reputation as the meanest, nastiest son of a bitch in Wisconsin. The only problem with this plan was that—though he would sooner kill his own mother than admit it—his brief encounter with his rival had made him question his ability to get the job done.

He supposed he could just run into the saloon and blow off Lewis' head with a shotgun before anyone had time to think about what was going on, but that would likely be considered a coward's move and would only work to further tarnish his reputation. No, if he wanted to go back to being the man everyone was afraid of, he would have to kill Lewis with his bare hands.

All he had to do was figure out a way to make sure that it wasn't a fair fight.

*   *   *

That year summer gave fall a pass and headed directly into winter, chilling the state with some of the coldest temperatures in living memory. It was the kind of cold that did more than raise goose bumps and induce shivers—it was the kind of cold that killed. On some days it got so bad that to go outside for longer than a few minutes without the right clothes was tantamount to suicide.

Leo McKillip was very happy. Unable to face the cold, many people were forced to stop in the small town and find shelter of some kind. With its enormous hearth kept burning 24 hours a day, McKillip's Saloon was busier than it had ever been before, but this boom in business did not come without a price.

As infamous as Evan was, he was still only one man and he had to sleep sometime. McKillip tried to help him by hiring other bouncers to take up the slack, but they all proved to be useless. For the first time since he had started, Evan was beginning to lose control of the saloon's clientele.

Still, money was money and his boss was willing to revert back to the way things used to be. More and more, Evan found himself unable to stop fights and having to settle with dealing with their aftermath. The ground was too cold for digging graves, so he and McKillip just stacked the bodies out back, where they awaited the spring thaw (the local sheriff having long since come to an agreement with

McKillip that his interest in such matters would only be aroused when a local townsperson became involved).

In his heart, Evan knew that unless something happened soon, the violence in the saloon would keep getting worse and worse until it reached a boiling point and something truly horrible happened.

His heart was right.

*   *   *

It was the coldest night of the year.

Evan was exhausted. He had been up for nearly 28 hours with only a few precious moments to sit down and rest. The customers were virtually trapped inside the saloon, and their inability to leave was causing a level of tension so dangerous that an army would have trouble keeping it at bay, much less one 16-year-old boy—no matter how big or strong he was.

During the last few hours he had stopped a dozen fights, all of which erupted instantly over the sort of incidents that would have gone unnoticed on a regular day. One fellow ended up being thrown onto the pile of frozen bodies out back because he had made the mistake of stepping on the toe of the wrong man. His card-playing murderer normally would have been thrown out of the bar, but McKillip knew that the gambler had a large wad a cash in his pocket and wanted the psychopathic gentleman to leave as much of it as possible at his establishment.

Evan knew that this leniency in the name of greed was making things even worse than they should have been, but nothing he said could convince his boss to change his mind.

"It's not like we're losing fine upstanding people here," McKillip defended his decision. "That fellow who died was no better than the man who killed him. What we have here is bastards killing bastards, and as long as the money is coming in I don't see any problem with it."

There was something almost defiant in the saloon owner's words, as if he was daring fate to spill innocent blood on his clean wooden floor.

At this point, though, Evan was too tired to care. His body could take only so much, and as more villains streamed into the saloon to escape the brutal cold, he slumped down into a chair and fell asleep.

In another corner of the saloon, a smile remained hidden under a heavy hood that obscured its wearer's face. Having heard about the establishment's gradual descent back to its old ways, Desmond Porter had come to the conclusion that now was the right time for him to get his revenge. The cold weather gave him an excuse to cover his extremely recognizable face, and he was able to walk into the saloon unnoticed. For several hours he just sat and watched his prey, waiting for the moment when Evan would be too weak to fight back.

Porter knew it would do his reputation no good if he attacked while the boy was still asleep, so he decided to wait until there was a commotion loud enough to wake him. Groggy and still tired, his defenses would be down and he could be killed in what would be grudgingly considered a fair fight by most observers.

It was only a matter of time before such a disturbance occurred, but Porter was growing impatient, and it didn't take him long to decide that he should just create one himself. All he had to do was figure out what it would be.

As he looked around for ideas, the door to the saloon opened, bringing a blast of freezing air with it. Heads turned as everyone looked to check out the new arrivals. No one said a word, but it was instantly clear to everyone that things were soon going to get very interesting.

The two boys could not have picked a worse place to escape the cold. They appeared to be brothers, about a year apart in their middle teens. Their clothes were old, torn and ragged—not at all suited to the weather outside. The fact that they willingly entered McKillip's Saloon proved that they weren't from around the area, and the blue tinge to their lips suggested that they had been out walking for a long time.

Before the two of them could figure out the precarious nature of their situation, they both saw the large fire burning in the saloon's enormous hearth. Their eyes grew wide at its warm beauty, and they ran to it with their arms outstretched. They could not believe their luck.

"I was so cold I thought I was going to die," said the slightly older boy.

"I was so cold I thought I *was* dead," said the other.

Sensing that something even he could not justify was about to happen, McKillip tried to scare the two boys away by shouting at them from his place behind the bar. "That fire's not for free, you know!" he told them, hoping they would get the hint and find shelter somewhere much safer for them. "If you want to stay you have to buy something to drink!"

The two boys looked at each other. "We only have enough money for a few drinks," worried the younger of the two.

"At this point I'm willing to give everything I have in this world for the warmth of this fire," his brother told him. "We'll have two coffees please," he turned and said to McKillip.

Before the saloon owner could say anything else, a quiet, yet audible gasp was heard coming from his regulars. There, in the far back corner of the room, a man had lowered his hood and revealed himself to be Empty Eye Porter. His presence now known, Porter stood up and approached the two young boys.

The younger of the two boys was still too entranced with the flames dancing in front of him to notice the almost demonically ugly stranger who was approaching them, but his brother was not. He turned and had to stop himself from audibly reacting to the horror that was Desmond Porter's face.

This was all Porter needed. "What are you looking at?" he sneered at the boy.

"Nothing, sir, nothing," the boy insisted as he quickly turned his gaze back toward the fire.

"Are you calling me nothing?" Porter roared at him.

In the other corner of the room, Evan was jerked awake by this sudden disturbance. His eyes still bleary with sleep, he looked up and saw what looked like Desmond Porter threatening a boy a year or two younger than himself. He tried to get up, but his body refused to listen to his mind and kept him planted in his chair. He was simply too tired to move.

"No sir!" the poor boy protested. "I just meant I wasn't looking at anything at all."

"Are you calling me a liar, boy?" Porter shouted with sadistic glee. "I may only have one eye, but it sees well enough to know when I'm being stared at!" He reached for the boy and grabbed him roughly by the shoulder.

"You leave him alone!" the boy's younger brother shouted at him.

Porter silenced him with a rough slap to the face, then turned back to the older boy. "If you're going to look at me," he said, "then look at me." With that he turned the boy so they were now face to face.

The boy cringed with fear. He looked around to the people surrounding them for any sign of rescue, but none appeared to be coming. No one was going to help him.

"What's the matter?" asked Porter. "Why do you keep squirming? Does my face disgust you? Am I the ugliest person you've ever seen?"

"No, sir," the boy shook his head. "You're as handsome as anybody!"

A roar of laughter filled the saloon as everyone in the room delighted in the desperation of the boy's lie.

"Leave him alone!" his younger brother repeated as he painfully lifted himself off of the floor. Porter slapped him again.

"Stay out of this!" his older brother shouted at him, not wanting to see him get any more hurt than he already was.

Back in the other corner of the room, Evan was fighting a war between his mind and his body. He knew he had to get up and stop what was happening before anyone was killed, but he had no strength left to do it. All he could do was watch, growing more anxious with each passing second.

"Look, sir," the older boy pleaded with Porter, "let us go and we'll leave right away. I promise! We just came in here to get out of the cold! We don't want any trouble!"

Porter smiled like a wild animal baring his teeth to prove how dangerous he was going to be in a fight. "But I do," he said, proving his words by smashing his forehead as hard he could into the boy's face.

The boy screamed with pain as blood rushed out of his nose. His brother got up from the floor and tried to jump onto Porter's back, but he was once again brought down by another hard slap to the face.

"And if you're so cold," Porter taunted the bleeding boy, "then why don't you let me warm you up a bit!"

Anyone in the saloon who had been enjoying this show thus far stopped when they saw what happened next. Right there in front of everyone, Porter grabbed the older boy and threw him into the fire.

The boy's screams echoed through the otherwise silent saloon. No one dared make a sound as the poor soul in front of them showed them the true meaning of hell. He scrambled out of the hearth, trying desperately to get out of his burning clothes and smother the flames that engulfed him, but it was no use. His skin began to bubble and burst as the smell of his roasting flesh and burnt hair began to make the people around him retch with disgust.

In the other corner of the room, the battle Evan had been fighting was won when he was forced to witness this horrible sight. The rage he felt powered his body with more energy than he had ever felt before. He jumped out his chair and moved toward Porter as fast as he could.

The one-eyed madman turned toward him and braced himself for the inevitable collision. He pulled out a long, sharp knife—the same one he had attempted to use in their last encounter—and aimed it for Evan's stomach.

Evan saw the knife and was able to avoid it as he threw the most powerful punch his right arm was capable of throwing. His fist connected directly with Porter's nose, causing a loud snapping sound that would have been heard by everyone were it not for the continued agony expressed by the burning boy's screams.

That one punch was all it took. In less than one second, the life in Desmond Porter's eyes faded away and his body fell to the floor. Lucy ran over to the burning boy with a blanket and threw it over his body, smothering the flames, but it was too late. He too was dead.

This left only the younger boy, who stared at the men surrounding him with a look of confusion and utter horror—as if his mind would not allow him to fully comprehend what he had just seen. Terrified, the boy jumped up and started running for the door.

"No, don't!" Evan shouted after him, afraid of what might happen if the boy went out alone on that cold, dark night. He tried to stop the boy by grabbing at the back of his coat, but the boy was so scared that he slipped out of the jacket and kept on running until he was out the door.

Evan chased after him, but a blizzard had begun to rage and it was impossible for him to see more than a few feet ahead of himself. The boy was gone and Evan was holding his only chance for survival.

They threw the bodies of Porter and the boy on top of the others in the frozen pile. Evan told McKillip that he quit, and—not wanting to stay there even a second longer—he faced the blizzard and returned home to his parents. They were very happy to see him, but they scolded him for being so foolish as to go outside on such a horrible night. He did not tell them why he felt he had no choice.

He warmed himself up with some hot cocoa and then went to his old bed and slept for two days straight.

When he woke up, he began to cry.

A week later he turned 17.

*   *   *

They found the younger boy's body frozen on the side of one the crossroads. His skin had turned blue and was covered with a thin layer of frost. As word spread across town and eventually reached Evan's ears, it was said that a look of ineffable terror was etched permanently on the poor child's face. When Evan's father told him this news, he stayed silent. In fact, he did not speak for several days. His guilt would not let him.

He had seen many horrible things during the brief time he had worked at the saloon, but the only images that haunted him were the faces of those two nameless boys. Although he had not killed them himself, they both died as a result of his actions. Had he not been so tired, he would have been able to stop Porter before he threw the boy into the fire. And—going back even further—had he not humiliated Porter so badly that first time they met, the one-eyed murderer might not have returned to the saloon looking for revenge, and both boys might have lived.

Evan told no one of the burden these thoughts had on his soul. Instead, he did his best to change the reputation he had earned when he had given in to the unfair expectations of his peers. He no longer cheated any of his father's customers, and he treated everyone with a friendliness that some found almost shocking in its intensity. Kindness seemed to be the easiest solution to the problem of how he was perceived—if at first people saw him as a devil, he would soon convince them that he was an angel.

It took time, but eventually everyone came to agree that they had long misjudged him. They began to think of him as a gentle giant—someone who made his presence known more through kindness than intimidation.

He never returned to the saloon or ever again spoke to any of the people who had—for a brief time—become his second family. He was glad when the place burned down in a fire that occurred the day after Christmas of 1839, but the story of how the blaze started caused a chill of fear to run down his spine. It was told to him by the town's sheriff, an educated man who had come to Ridgeway by way of Manchester, England, who had himself heard it from the fire's sole survivor.

"I tell you, Evan," the sheriff said with a weary shake of his head, "I have never seen as pathetic a sight as that old girl standing in front of that wretched little tavern as it burned to the ground. Said her name was Lucy—perhaps you knew her back during that time you worked there?"

"I don't think so," said Evan, not sure why he didn't want to admit that he had.

"These great big tears kept streaming down her face, and at first I thought it was because of the loss of her livelihood or some of the people left inside, but the more I talked to her, the more I realized that she had been traumatized by something else entirely. When she began talking she refused to admit to me what it was. She thought I would think her insane, and I don't blame her now that I've heard what she had to say. Perhaps she is mad, but I've never seen anyone speak with so much conviction in all my life. I can't help but believe her, despite what my common sense is telling me."

"What did she say?"

"She told me that the fire was not the work of any man, nor was it an accident. She told me that it was an act of revenge by the spirits of two boys who died the day they made the mistake of walking into that vile establishment."

"What?" asked Evan, his face turning pale as he spoke.

"Apparently it happened the night of that horrible blizzard. These two boys who no one had ever seen before came into the saloon to get out of the cold and were attacked by one of the sadistic regulars. She told me that he threw one of the boys into the fire and that the other escaped before he too was killed, but it is likely that he was the poor child that was found frozen on the side of the road just a few miles away from the saloon. Do you know anything about this?"

"No," Evan lied.

"Perhaps she made it all up, but she was dead certain that just before the saloon caught on fire she saw the spirits of the two boys walk through its doors. She told me that they looked upon everyone with gazes of pure hatred, and then the spirit of the older boy—the one she said had been burned alive—burst into flame and set the building on fire. She told me that everyone inside tried to run for the door, but the spirit of the younger boy transformed into a large, vicious dog and kept them away with the threat of its enormous fangs. She was the only person he let pass, owing—she believed—to the fact that she had been the one to try and save his brother by putting out the flames that killed him. Everyone else perished—suffering the same painful death they did nothing to stop that winter night. Can you believe that, Evan? Do you honestly think such a thing could really happen?"

"I hope not," was all Evan could say.

"So do I," said the sheriff, "but if it's true then I can only wish one thing."

"What's that?"

"That these two spirits are appeased and no longer have any desire for revenge."

In his heart Evan knew that the sheriff's wish would not be granted, and his heart was right again. The wrath of these two spirits had not ended—it had just begun.

*   *   *

The New Year arrived, and 1840 was only a few days old when Evan started hearing reports of travelers along the Ridgeway crossroads having strange encounters that they could not explain away rationally. As the months passed, the frequency of these stories grew until no one could deny that something truly spooky was occurring along those roadways.

What convinced all but the most stubborn of skeptics was the uniformity of these tales—the same story was heard over and over again, even though it was most frequently told by folks who had no previous awareness of the dangers the roads presented to anyone who traveled them. Evan heard one of these tales straight from the source when he went into the town's general store one Monday morning to buy some groceries. He was paying for his purchases when a distraught-looking man ran into the store and asked the owner where he could find the local lawman.

"I have seen something wicked out on the road this night," the man told them, "and the sheriff should be warned of it."

"What did you see?" asked Evan.

"I want to tell you," said the man, "as it was one of those experiences that a man must speak of if only to warn others so that they do not face it themselves, but you will think I—"

"We will think no such thing," said Evan. "The people here have become well aware that strange things happen out on the crossroads at night."

"Then you know!" said the man. "I was afraid that I had lost my mind, but the experience was so real I have no choice but to believe that I did not dream it and that it did occur."

"You dreamed nothing," said Evan. "What did you see?"

"I was out on the road, alone on my horse. I could see the town in the distance and had decided to seek out a room for the night. Along the way I saw two boys standing in the middle of the road. They had to be brothers because they were the spitting image of one another, though if I had to guess I would say that they were not twins. Even from a distance I could tell that there was something more than a little strange about the two of them. I had to rub my eyes for fear that they were deceiving me, but it appeared that one of the boys was emanating strong, thick wisps of smoke from his body while the other had skin that was an icy shade of blue. I called out to them, but they did not seem to hear me. As I came closer I saw that they were both possessed with the most frightening of expressions—it was clear that there was evil in their hearts and that they meant to do me harm. I dug my heals into my horse's sides and started riding at a full gallop so I could pass by them as quickly as I could, but as I started to race past them they—" the man stopped, unprepared to fully describe what he had seen them do next. "They," he continued hesitantly, "transformed themselves before my eyes and took on the shapes of a large, demonic dog and a ball of white flame. I myself find it nearly impossible to believe it, but I swear that is what I saw! I raced my horse as fast as the poor animal could run, but its speed was no match for the two demons—I ask you, sirs, how do you outrun a ball of fire? It was too much for my animal, and its right hind leg shattered from the exertion. I was thrown into the air and landed on my back. I must have had my senses knocked out of me, because the next thing I remember, the sun was rising in the sky and the monsters that had chased me were gone. My poor horse lay on the ground in utter agony, and I had to shoot it so its misery would cease. After that I walked here wanting to warn the local lawman of what happened to me, but if what you say is true and I am not the first man to tell such a tale, then I doubt there is anything he can do."

*   *   *

Over the course of the next six years, Evan's parents both passed on and he inherited the family business. The combination of his size and gentle demeanor made him very popular with Ridgeway's young ladies, and he was able to marry the beautiful daughter of the town's local physician. They had two children who both showed signs of inheriting their father's size and their mother's good looks. It appeared to everyone who knew him that he was as happy as any man could ever expect to be, but in his own mind he always knew that one day he would meet the devils that haunted the crossroads, and his happiness would forever come to an end.

Thus far he had done a masterful job of avoiding those crossroads, knowing that if the spirits of the two murdered boys were content to strike at complete strangers, then there was no telling what they would do to someone who actually deserved their vengeance. Still, he knew some day he would have to face them, and he would pay the ultimate price when he did.

*   *   *

In 1874, Evan was 50 years old and a very highly respected member of his community. It had been so long since he had lost his reputation as a bully that few people even remembered it. Even fewer remembered the nasty old saloon that had burned down all those years ago, but no one had forgotten the spirits of the two angry young boys that still haunted the town's crossroads.

For 34 years Evan had managed to steer clear of the Ridgeway Phantoms, as they had become known, and during those years he had heard many more horrifying stories that told of what happened to others who were not so lucky. He heard of one fellow who saw them transform into a herd of monstrous pigs, and another who was chased for miles when they attacked him as two shadowy black steeds whose eyes burned with a malevolent redness. But most of the stories matched the one told by the stranger Evan had met in the general store, in which the two phantoms took on the guises of a hellhound and a giant white ball of fire. Too many of these stories existed for them not to be true.

But fate can only wait so long before it forces the inevitable to occur, and on May 6 of that year, Evan came face to face with his worst fears.

The incident that allowed for this long-awaited meeting was almost as bizarre as the meeting itself. Despite the absence of McKillip's Saloon, Ridgeway still managed to attract nefarious types. Among these criminals were two drifters named Green and Owens who had spent several days noting which businesses seemed to be doing the most brisk business, and which would therefore be the best to rob. It didn't take them long to decide that the town's butcher shop was a perfect target. It was only the sight of the butcher himself, all six feet five inches of him, that caused the two men to hesitate in going forward with their plan.

"Have you seen the size of those hands?" Owens asked his partner. "Not to mention those knives he's got with him!"

"But that's only a problem if he's there," said Green. "If we rob the place at night, he won't be there to turn us into hamburger."

"I suppose," Owens said reluctantly, "but what if he turns up?"

"I don't care how big the man is," said his partner, "if I shoot him with this," he held up the revolver he had successfully stolen from a gambler in the last town they were in, "he's going to go down."

That night the two men broke into the butcher shop and discovered, to their disappointment, that it contained no cash. Evan had been robbed once before and no longer kept any on site after closing time.

"Dammit!" Green swore after an exhaustive search of the premises failed to turn up even a spare penny. "Well," he sighed, "there must be something in this place that's worth stealing."

"I know some fellas who could probably use those knives and cleavers," said Owens. "I'm sure they're plenty good in a fight."

"Grab 'em," said his partner. "I'll see if he has any steaks hanging around."

As their big heist turned into a desperate looting, the two thieves had no idea that the man they had been afraid of was doing something he almost never did—returning to the store in the middle of the night.

That night Evan had slipped into his bed and was just about to go to sleep when his mind flashed back to the oil lamps he had lit while he was working in the windowless back room. He remembered blowing all but one of them out before he left, and he became worried about what could happen if he hadn't blown out the last one. It was likely that the oil would simply run out and the flame would burn out on its own. But it was also possible that the flame was still burning, and if something caused the lamp to fall from its perch, his entire business could go up in flames.

He knew he would probably regret it, but he decided that the only way he was going to get any sleep would be if he got up and went to the store to check to see that it was still there and not simply a pile of ash and cinders.

The store was still there when he arrived, but to his surprise he found that its front door had been jimmied open.

He walked inside and saw two men filling their arms with his goods in the dim light of their own oil lamps. Before he could say anything, one of them pulled out a revolver and pulled its trigger twice. Evan felt a sharp pain in his left arm that caused him to fall. His head hit the wooden floor with a loud thud, and he did not move.

"Is he dead?" asked Owens.

"I dunno," admitted Green. "He sure looks dead, and I shot him twice."

He actually only shot Evan once; the other bullet had whizzed past the butcher's head and out the front door, where it was eventually stopped by the door of the building across the street.

"What do we do with him? Should we just leave him here? If he's not dead and he wakes up, he could identify us," worried Owens.

Green wasn't used to thinking this hard, and the strain was starting to show. "Pick up his feet," he ordered his partner. "I'll take his head."

"Where are we going to take him?"

"In the back of our wagon. We'll ride until we're miles out of town and then we'll dump his body on the side of the road. If he's dead it won't matter, and if he isn't it'll be hours before he can talk to anybody, and by then we'll be long gone."

"That's smart," said Owens.

It wasn't, but it was the best Green could do. Unfortunately, Evan's weight and the two men's inability to bear it proved to be a barrier in making it happen.

"I think I saw a wheel barrow in the back," said Green. "Go get it."

Owens nodded and returned a minute later with the wheelbarrow Evan used for the sides of beef that were so heavy even he had trouble lifting them. The two hapless crooks managed to lift him up long enough to get him into the device, which they rolled to their wagon. It then took all of their strength to lift him up and throw him onto the back of their buckboard.

"He's got to be dead," said Owens as they went back to the store to get their loot, "because we sure would have woken him doing all of that if he wasn't."

Owens' theory grew increasingly plausible as they rode for an hour and Evan showed no sign of waking. Green decided they were finally far enough out of the town to get rid of their passenger, so they dumped Evan's body on the side of the road and continued on with their stolen knives and meat.

Another hour passed and Evan slowly opened his eyes. As he awoke, his first thought wasn't the pain in his arm or the goods that had been stolen from him, but the terrifying realization that he was laying beside one the Ridgeway crossroads. After three and a half decades of avoiding these roads they had finally claimed him, and he knew what they were going to do with him.

It turned out that the wound on his left arm was minor and didn't hurt half as much as his head, which still throbbed from the pain caused by its hard introduction to the butcher shop's floor. It was dark, and the moon was only a small sliver in the sky, so he could barely see a foot in front of his face. What he could see was doubled, another result of the injury to his head. He could barely stand up, let alone walk, but fear is a powerful motivator, and at that moment it was compelling Evan to get back home as fast as he could.

There was just one problem. He had no idea where he was, thanks to the combination of darkness and the fact that—having avoided the crossroads for most of his life—he knew virtually nothing about the areas outside of Ridgeway. He also had no idea how long he had been unconscious or how far the two thieves had ridden before they dumped him on the side of the road. As far he knew, he could be 10 minutes away from his home or 10 hours. He didn't even know in which direction he should walk. All he did know was that he had to keep moving—he could not bear to think of what would happen to him if he stayed in one place.

Purely by chance, he started moving in the right direction. His legs wobbled beneath him, but he managed to walk without falling. His injuries were starting to make him feel nauseated, and he had to stop twice to vomit along the way. He walked for an hour, seeing nothing that indicated he was getting anywhere closer to his home. By that time he had become so consumed with the effort it took to not simply collapse on the ground and go to sleep that he had nearly forgotten what was compelling him to keep moving in the first place.

All it took was the sudden sensation of unexpected warmth to remind him. As his right arm swung back behind him, his hand felt the hot air of another creature's breath.

He did not look back. He knew what was there.

Just seconds ago he could barely walk and was on the verge of collapse, but now he found himself possessed with the strength to run faster than he had ever ran before.

Although he did not look back, he could feel the presence of the animal running behind him. He could tell it was a massive animal, stronger than any other dog that ever lived and capable of ripping the flesh from his bones as easily as a man eating a cooked chicken wing.

Evan ran for what felt like hours but was really only a few minutes. The point came when even the worst fear in the world couldn't keep his enormous body moving. His lungs burned and his legs were knotted with cramps—the pain was too much; he couldn't continue.

Knowing his end had come, he stopped and finally turned around.

And saw nothing.

Nothing was there.

He was alone.

Tears came to his eyes as his legs gave out from under him and he fell to his knees. He couldn't tell if they were tears of pain or relief.

Unable to move any further, he lay down on the ground and closed his eyes.

When he opened them again it was still dark. He was so delirious he could not tell if he had been unconscious for just a few minutes—and sunrise was just moments away—or if he had been so exhausted that he had lain there the entire day and a new night had fallen.

Whichever the case, he felt as though he could get up. He stood up slowly and started walking, still not sure if he was headed in the right direction.

He had lost all sense of time, and he began to pray for the sun to rise, knowing that the spirits of the two boys only attacked travelers at night. At last it appeared that his prayers had finally been answered when light began to appear behind him. He turned to look at it and saw that the light was not from the rising sun, but from a giant ball of white fire floating up above him.

It was possible he had merely imagined the dog, but there was no imagining this. The heat of the ball's flames burned against his skin, and though he knew it was futile to run, he turned around and did it anyway.

This time, as the ball of fire chased him, he somehow managed the miracle of running even faster than he had before. Knowing for certain what was behind him, he couldn't help but look back as he ran. As he did he saw that the ball of fire was not alone. Below it he saw the hell-hound that had chased him earlier. He had not imagined it; it was very real, and evidently the two spirits were toying with him, choosing to lengthen his misery as long they could before finally deciding to strike.

But as he ran, Evan began to laugh because he could see, in the distance, that their games had come with a price. The sun was now really rising, bringing the end of the night with it. As it appeared over the horizon, the two spirits faded away, and he saw that he was only a short run away from the road that led into Ridgeway—he was nearly home.

But he would not get there.

A person's body can only take so much so exertion, especially a body as big as Evan's. His heart had been pushed to the brink and there was no going back. Before he could leave the crossroads, it exploded in his chest and his body dropped to the ground and lay there dead until it was discovered a few hours later.

No one said it at his funeral, but everyone knew he was a victim of the Ridgeway Phantoms. What none of them knew was why.

*   *   *

The reign of terror of these two vengeful spirits did not end with the death of the last man who had been in McKillip's Saloon the day they were so cruelly murdered for the crime of wanting to get out of the cold. They continued to haunt the crossroads for another 36 years, but then in 1910 a fire reduced most of Ridgeway to a pile of ash.

It was claimed by some who survived this disaster that they saw two teenaged boys looking out a window of one of the burning buildings, both of them grinning from ear to ear as the flames devoured the entire town. Whether or not this was true, one thing was certain—after that day, the spirits of those two boys were never seen again.

Taliesin

In the town of Spring Green, Wisconsin, is a building that transcends the boundaries of architecture into the realm of high art. Nothing less could be expected from a house that once served as the home of America's—if not the world's—most famous architect, Frank Lloyd Wright. He called it Taliesin (pronounced Tally-ess-in) in honor of the earliest known Welsh poet, whose name means "shining bow." The house was built in the valley that had been settled by his mother's parents, where he had spent his adolescent summers learning the ideals and values that he carried with him for the rest of his life.

The building has been described as his "sketch pad" because it was there that he tried out all of his ideas before he implemented them in other buildings. It is because of this experimentation that Taliesin could be described as the archetypal Wright building—the one that most clearly defined his artistic vision and architectural philosophy. He used it to further the cause of "organic" architecture, in which a building is designed to be harmonious with its natural surroundings. The goal is to have the building appear almost as if it grew out of the ground ready to be lived in, while at the same time expressing the qualities of youth, playfulness and joyful discovery. Built with limestone and stucco walls that had been mixed with sand from the nearby Wisconsin River, Taliesin does indeed appear as though it sprouted fully formed from the hillside on which Wright built it. As a result, it is a place that inspires a feeling of peace and calm in almost everyone who visits it.

The great irony of this glorious structure is that such a calm and peaceful building became site of one of Wisconsin's most grisly crimes, the spiritual effects of which can still be felt there today, over 90 years after that crime occurred.

For all of its tranquility and beauty, Taliesin is a building haunted by its past, and it is likely going to stay that way for as long as it exists.

*   *   *

When Wright started building Taliesin his life was in turmoil—but that was normal for him. His was a life lived dangerously close to the edge; he tested the limits of his own personal breaking points far more than any normal man would care to.

In 1904—when he was 37 and living in the town of Oak Park, Illinois—he was hired to design a home for a neighbor of his named Edwin Cheney. It was through this work that he met Cheney's wife, a beautiful woman with the unusual name of Mamah. Although Wright had by that time been married to his wife Kitty for over a decade, he found himself instantly attracted to his client's wife. He soon discovered that the attraction was mutual, and it didn't take long for rumors of their affair to spread throughout their small community. Over the course of the next five years he and his lover tried to convince their spouses to grant them divorces so they could be together, but both Edwin and Kitty refused.

Finally, Wright and Mamah could not wait any longer. They abandoned their families to go to Europe together. They stayed there for two years, during which time Edwin eventually divorced Mamah—a concession Kitty adamantly refused to duplicate. Unable to marry the love of his life, Wright returned to the United States while Mamah made a home for herself in Fiezole, Italy.

Because Kitty retained ownership of their home in Oak Park, Wright was in the position of having to find a new place to live once he came back to America. Remembering the summers he had spent with his mother's family in the valley of Spring Green, Wisconsin, he decided that that was the perfect place to build his new home.

The building he designed was made up of three wings: one to serve as his professional studio, another for farm work and a third to serve as his living space. It was ready for him and Mamah, who had by then dropped her ex-husband's surname in favor of her maiden name, Borthwick, to move in to just before Christmas of 1911.

Although Kitty's obstinacy still kept them from getting married, the two of them lived happily in Taliesin for three years until a horrible crime ended their scandalous love affair once and for all.

Wright was working in Chicago when Mamah decided to fire the butler he had hired a few months earlier. Julian Carlton was a man whose temper proved a little too fiery for Mamah's comfort. She had grown fearful of his outbursts and decided it was in their best interest to get rid of him before he did something truly violent.

Unfortunately, it was precisely this move that sent Carlton over the edge. After he was told that he was fired, he left the house, but he soon returned with a lit torch and an ax. Using the torch he set Taliesin's residential wing on fire and then proceeded to kill everyone he saw inside with the ax.

Mamah and her two children, John, 11 years old, and Martha, 9 years old, were murdered. Also killed in the attack were Emil Brodelle, one of Wright's draftsmen; a gardener named David Lindblom; a hostler named Thomas Brunker; and Ernest Weston, the 13-year-old son of Taliesin's foreman, William Weston. The senior Weston was one of only two people who survived the vicious attack; the other survivor was a guest from Chicago named Herbert Fritz, who broke his arm while fleeing from the burning building. Together the two men ran half a mile to the home of Wright's nearest neighbors, the Reiders, where they telephoned for help. Although the office and farm wings of the house were spared from the fire, the residential wing was completely destroyed.

Wright's terrible grief was only compounded by the newspaper stories that followed the massacre. Many of them seem far more interested in the details of his personal life than the death of his loved ones. He was forced to read over and over again as Mamah—the woman he considered to truly be his wife—was described as his mistress, with some articles going so far as to implicitly suggest that the murders were a karmic result of the couple's adultery.

Few of the news stories bothered to say anything about the man who committed these horrible murders. Many people who read these stories never learned that following his killing spree, Carlton tried to commit suicide by drinking acid, but this choice proved an inefficient method of self-annihilation. He lingered in prison for eight days before he finally died.

Wright rebuilt Taliesin and was eventually freed from his marriage to Kitty in 1922, which allowed him to marry a woman named Miriam Noel in 1923, but that marriage lasted less than a year owing to the strain caused by her addiction to morphine. In 1928, after a four-year court-ship that was nearly as traumatic as the one he had shared with Mamah, he married Olga Hinzenburg. During that time Taliesin experienced not one but two more fires, both of which left damages that were very expensive to repair. In 1937 he built a home in Scottsdale, Arizona, which he dubbed Taliesin West. From that point on he alternated between the two Taliesins, staying in Spring Green in the warmer months of the year and in Scottsdale during win-ter. By the time he died in 1959, at the age of 91, he had earned a reputation as the most important and influential architect of his time—a reputation many believe still holds up today.

Following his death, the original Taliesin became a National Historical Landmark and is taken care of by the Frank Lloyd Wright Foundation, an organization he founded with his third wife, Olga, in the 1940s. It is a place dedicated to preserving the memory of his professional legacy, but anyone who visits one particular small cottage on the property has a good chance of coming face-to-face with a memory from his private life as well.

Following the call made by William Weston and Herbert Fritz at the home of the Reiders after they had escaped from Julian Carlton's rampage, a group of fire-fighters descended upon Taliesin and extinguished the blaze. They then discovered that several of Carlton's vic-tims—including a very badly burned Mamah—were not yet dead. They were taken to a small cottage on the estate's grounds called Tan-Y-Deri, where they all eventually suc-cumbed to their wounds.

Since that time the spirit of Wright's murdered lover has haunted this small cottage, where she is seen either wearing a long white gown or washing clothes—a chore she found relaxing. Other signs of her presence include doors and windows opening and then slamming shut without apparent cause, as well as the occasional unexplainable smell of smoke in the air.

Those who have seen her describe a spirit who is unusually gentle and calm, considering the cause of her death. She appears to harbor no grudge against the world that tried to deny her a life with the man she loved.

Without any visible signs of anger or regret, it is hard to understand why her spirit would choose to linger in the spot where she died for as long as it has. Perhaps it is waiting for something that may never come, such as the spirit of her long-dead lover, not knowing that he had 41 years to get over her loss and move on—a benefit of time fate did not allow her to share.

The Griffon

René-Robert Cavelier, Sieur de La Salle, was a French adventurer who spent most of his life exploring early America. Instrumental in the establishment of the fur trade, he is best remembered today not for his achievements, but for his greatest disaster. Out around Washington Island, which is found in Wisconsin's Green Bay Harbor, the ghostly remnant of his enormous loss can still be seen lurking in the fog that clouds those waters.

La Salle's life was filled with enormous peaks and valleys—the kinds of highs and lows that only truly extraordinary men can ever hope to experience. Born in the town of Rouen, France, on November 22, 1643, he decided early on in life that he wanted to live a life in the church. At the age of 17 he joined the Jesuit order and stayed with them for seven years until he asked to leave, insisting that his moral weaknesses kept him from truly being worthy of priesthood.

He left the Jesuit order without a penny to his name. As part of his indoctrination into the society he had been required to give up the inheritance that was his following his father's death. Still, he was able to find passage to North America, where he joined his brother Jean in New France. At that time, property in the French colonies was divided into what were called *seigneuries*. They were long strips of land owned by the King of France that were given over to specific individuals to care for. La Salle was given a seigneurie on the western end of the Island of Montreal. The strip of land became known as Lachine, which some have suggested was meant to mock La Salle and his attempts to discover a new route to Asia (Lachine being derived from La Chine, the French name for China).

Having been granted the land, La Salle moved there and set up a village, and it was there that he first encountered the Iroquois people. A gifted linguist, La Salle learned their language and from them first heard about the Ohio River. Believing that this river flowed into the Gulf of California and thus offered a convenient route to Asia, he decided to sell his investments in Lachine to finance an expedition to first find and then travel along it.

In 1669 he set out with 15 men in five canoes. He found the Ohio River and traveled all the way to what would eventually become Louisville, Kentucky, before he was forced to give up the venture.

Four years later, in 1673, La Salle was instrumental in establishing Fort Frontenac (in the future city of Kingston, Ontario), a key site in the burgeoning fur trade. It was thanks to this effort that he received a valuable fur trade concession from the king, as well as a title of nobility. After six years at the fort, La Salle decided he was ready to once again explore the New World. This time he was able to finance an operation far larger than five canoes. Using the fortune he had amassed trading furs, he built the *Griffon*, a 60-foot-long sailing ship that weighed 45 tons and came equipped with five guns.

The *Griffon* wasn't the first ship La Salle had built. The first, a 10-ton vessel he named *Le Frontenac*, sank in Lake Ontario on January 8, 1679. It wouldn't be long before the *Griffon* followed suit.

The large ship, the first of its kind to sail on the upper Great Lakes, started its first voyage on August 7, 1679, launching from the Niagara River. It sailed across lakes Erie,

Huron and Michigan before arriving in Green Bay Harbor, where it docked at Washington Island. From there La Salle left his ship and went on a canoeing expedition down the St. Joseph River in search of a way to reach the mighty Mississippi. He was joined by all but six of the *Griffon*'s 34-man crew. The six men that remained on the sailing ship followed La Salle's orders and left Green Bay Harbor on September 18 of that same year.

Neither those men nor the *Griffon* were ever seen again.

Nobody knew what happened to the ship during its journey back to the Niagara. All anyone could be sure of was that it never got there and must have been lost somewhere along the Great Lakes.

Undeterred by the loss, La Salle kept on exploring the New World. Three years after the *Griffon*'s disappearance, he canoed down the Mississippi River with a crew of 23 Frenchmen and 18 Native Americans. When he reached the river's basin, he named it Louisiana after the King of France. He then proceeded to claim the land in the name of the king.

In 1684 he followed this achievement by gathering together a large expedition with which he planned to establish a new colony on the Gulf of Mexico. This adventure would prove to be his most difficult. Slowed down by pirates, unfriendly locals and poor planning, the expedition had lost three ships by the time it reached what would become Texas. There the expedition landed and La Salle and his crew set out on foot to find the Mississippi River, which they hoped would take them back home. The first two attempts to find the river were unsuccessful, but nowhere near as disastrous as the third. During this final trek, La Salle's men had enough of what they perceived as his incompetence, and they started a mutiny that led to his being murdered by four of his own crewmembers.

It was only after La Salle's death that people started hearing rumors about mysterious sightings of a phantom vessel that bore a strong resemblance to his largest and most famous ship. It was also around this time that a story started being told that the *Griffon* had not disappeared randomly but had in fact been cursed even before it first set sail.

According to the story, when the completed ship was first set down upon the waters of the Niagara, it was seen by a Iroquois prophet named Metiomek, who was shocked and offended by the size of it.

"That ship mocks the Great Spirit," Metiomek insisted. "Its dimensions are an offence to all that is natural, and it cannot be abided. If we allow this vessel to travel across the water, the Great Spirit will think that we approve of his humiliation and will bring ruin down upon us all. If we are to save ourselves, we must curse the ship and ensure that its mockery comes to an end."

True to his words, Metiomek cursed the ship. "You may now be vast," he spoke as he performed the ritual that would doom the *Griffon*, "but your size will mean nothing when you are but a shadow. You want to travel across the water? Then you shall do so forever. You will never be able to stop or allow the men who guide you to return to the land they abandoned once they set foot on you."

At first Metiomek thought his curse had failed, but when the ship failed to return home from its voyage, he knew that it had succeeded.

If this story was true and the phantom ship that was becoming a frequent sight on the waters of Green Bay Harbor really was the *Griffon*, why then did it take five years after the ship disappeared for it to reappear again in ghostly form?

It soon became popular opinion that the answer to this question was that the ship was waiting for the man who built it to return to it.

Metiomek had cursed the ship and all of its crewmembers, including La Salle, but when it disappeared only six of those men were actually onboard. It was believed that as those crewmembers who escaped their cursed fate started dying, their spirits returned to the *Griffon* to man its sails for the rest of eternity. Once La Salle was murdered by his own men, his spirit was fair game for the curse to ensnare. It brought him back to his lost ship, where he would now forever serve as its captain.

But just because this opinion is popular does not mean everyone agrees with it. Some who have actually seen the *Griffon* sail through the fog of Green Bay Habor insist that they saw no sign of any men aboard it. They insist that it has no crew to guide it, which is why it cannot leave the harbor and go on to other waters.

One hopes that these folks are right and that only the *Griffon* has been cursed to sail the waters of Green Bay for the past three centuries and into eternity. It can feel no loneliness, no sense of loss. It is simply doing what it does, what it had been built to do. But the same cannot be said for the spirits of the men who might still be connected to it. If they are still on the boat then they have been at sail for over 300 years, which is far too long for even the most ardent of lifelong sailors.

René-Robert Cavelier, Sieur de La Salle, did not live a perfect life and made many mistakes along with his successes, but that does not justify such a horrible fate. If you are sailing on the waters of Wisconsin's most famous harbor and you see a very old boat in the distant fog, you should ignore it—for a curse can only exist as long as people keep on acknowledging its existence.

2
Haunted Men

The Factory

"So what brings you to La Crosse?" Nils asked Porter, the new guy.

It seemed like a simple question, but Porter chose to think about it before he supplied his answer. "I'm not sure," he admitted. "I just sort of ended up here, I guess. It wasn't like I planned it."

"How do you like it?"

"It's a town," he shrugged. "They're all pretty much the same."

"I suppose," Nils said politely, even though his civic pride was insulted by his new partner's unenthusiastic response. He thought La Crosse was the greatest town in the whole world, which was why he had never even attempted to travel anywhere else.

"So what is it that we're supposed to do exactly?" asked Porter. "The guy who hired me wasn't very clear about that. Please don't tell me it involves a lot of heavy lifting."

"Why?" asked Nils. "Do you have a bad back?"

"No," Porter shook his head, "I'm just lazy."

This made Nils laugh and softened his opinion of the fellow, who at least had a good sense of humor. "Then this is the perfect job for you," he smiled. "All we're supposed to do is walk around the factory and make sure that no thieves or saboteurs break in and wreak all sorts of havoc."

"Saboteurs?" asked Porter. "At a door factory?"

"Don't you kid yourself," Nils answered. "The George Pierce Sash and Door Factory has many rivals who would be more than happy to see that our machinery ceased to function."

"Name one."

"Well…uh…other door factories, I suppose. There have to be plenty out there. I couldn't tell you where exactly, but I'm sure they're around and would be perfectly happy to see us go out of business."

"So what are we supposed to do if we do happen to run into a thief or a," Porter allowed himself a small smile before he said the word, "saboteur?"

"Stop and catch him, I suppose," answered Nils. "Truthfully, it's never been an issue. We don't have much crime in La Crosse," he said proudly.

"Because there's nothing in this place that's worth stealing," Porter whispered under his breath. It wasn't just a slur against the town, but a professional insight. Porter was a thief by trade, and thus far he had found little in La Crosse that was worth his time. He had been about to leave for a more lucrative location when he heard about the door factory's payroll, which was kept overnight in the factory's safe every Wednesday night before being distributed to the employees Thursday morning. It was now Monday, which gave him two days to find the safe and figure out if he could crack it. He didn't think Nils would prove too difficult an obstacle.

"What was that?" asked Nils.

"Pardon?"

"I thought I heard you say something under your breath."

"Oh, I said, 'I knew when I came here that this town had a very safe feeling,'" he lied.

"It sure does," Nils smiled. "It sure does."

"Are there any spots we have to give more attention to than others?" Porter changed the subject.

"Just Mr. Dickens' office," answered Nils. "He's the company accountant, and his office is where the factory safe is."

"That *does* sound important," said Porter. "Maybe you should show me where that is first."

"Sure," said Nils, "that's as good a place as any for us to start. It's up the stairs where all of the other offices are located."

"Lead the way, my friend, lead the way," Porter urged him.

"You really are an eager fellow, aren't you?" asked Nils.

"Eager as a beaver, Nils," Porter smiled at him.

"Than let's go," Nils laughed before he started walking toward the upstairs offices.

"Finally…" Porter sighed from behind him.

"What was that?" Nils stopped and turned around to ask him.

"Finally…uh…" Porter improvised, "I can start earning my wages."

"Oh," said Nils. If he seemed at all suspicious, he was very good at hiding it. He turned back around and the two of them walked up the stairs in silence. Nils' thoughts were occupied by visions of the lunch his wife had packed for him, while Porter wondered how difficult it would be to knock out and tie up the large man in front of him this upcoming Wednesday night.

"This is Mr. Dickens' office," Nils informed Porter as they reached a door at the end of the upstairs hallway. "And this," he held up a key from the chain that was attached to one of his belt loops, "is the key to get us inside."

Porter studied the key and memorized its shape. Knowing which one it was would save him some time. Nils opened the door and the two of them held up their lamps to bring some much-needed light to the dark room.

"There's the safe," Nils told Porter as he pointed to the safe-shaped object in the far-right corner of the room. "Take a look at it, if you want. It's a fancy model that Mr. Pierce had shipped in from New York City. All of the important Wall Street types use it for their businesses."

Porter walked over to the safe and had to stop himself from doing a jig of happiness when he saw it up close. He had seen this particular model many times in the course of his career, and he could have it open in 10 minutes—half that if he really concentrated.

"Impressive, isn't it?" asked Nils. "I bet you won't find a safe like that in Madison or Green Bay," he speculated, saying the names of those other Wisconsin towns with a tone that made them sound like they were Sodom and Gomorrah.

"Madison had one," Porter said to himself.

"Pardon me?" asked Nils. "You do mumble a lot, don't you?"

"Sorry," Porter apologized.

"It's nothing for you to be concerned about," Nils told him. "A lot of people mumble. They weren't raised by someone like my mother, who was a stickler for perfect diction. What was that?"

"Excuse me?" asked Porter.

"I felt something drip onto my forehead," explained Nils. He lifted a finger to the spot and touched it. He then studied his finger with the help of his lamp. "It's blood," he exclaimed, shocked by such a bizarre discovery. He then held his lamp up and turned his gaze to the ceiling. Porter joined him, and the combined wattage of their lamps allowed them to see a dark red stain above their heads. They then watched as another droplet of blood gathered together and dropped to the floor at their feet.

"What's above this room?" asked Porter.

"An attic, I think," answered Nils. "Whatever it is, no one has used it for anything in years. I've never even been up there."

"It's time to change that, I think," Porter told him.

"I suppose you're right," agreed Nils.

The stairway to the abandoned attic was protected by a door that Nils hadn't seen opened once in the decade he had worked at the factory, which was why he was surprised to discover it ajar when he and Porter approached it.

"I thought I had the only key that opened this door," he told Porter. "I guess I was wrong. I wonder who else would have one?"

"Only one way to find out," said Porter. "You go first and I'll watch your back."

Nils frowned and started walking up the stairs, each step imitating the creaking cackle of an old witch as he made his way. Slowly and hesitantly, Porter followed him.

"Watch out for the cobwebs," warned Nils. "There're a lot of them."

Unfortunately for Porter this warning came too late, as he had already gotten a face full of dusty old web, most of which went into his mouth. He soon became so distracted by his attempts to spit out the taste of the web that he failed to notice when they reached the top of the stairs and entered the old, unused attic.

"I didn't realize it was this big," said Nils. "Seems like an awful waste of space not to use it for something. Even just to store boxes or something like that."

Porter was still too busy sputtering to respond.

"I suppose what we're looking for is all the way at the other end, if the blood dripping into Mr. Dickens' office is anything to go by," Nils continued.

Porter had finally succeeded in clearing the taste of cobweb out of his mouth, and he noted the surprising bravery of the man he was with—he had written him off as an oaf. "Aren't you frightened?" he asked Nils as they walked to the other end of the attic.

"Why should I be?" Nils shrugged in the darkness.

"Because we're investigating the cause of the big pool of blood that is dripping down through the ceiling, which could very easily be something we don't want to find."

"Ah, don't be so over-imaginative," said Nils. "It's just a raccoon or cat that got trapped up here and died trying to—" but before he could finish this thought the light from his lamp caught sight of something hanging from the rafters above them.

Both men screamed at the same time.

There, hanging from a noose made out of barbed wire, was the body of a middle-aged man.

"Who is that?" asked Porter, his voice still hoarse from his screaming.

"It's Mr. Dickens," answered Nils. "Or, at least, it used to be."

*   *   *

Porter waited alone in the factory while his partner raced to inform the town's sheriff and Mr. Pierce, the factory's owner, about their grisly discovery. The telephone had yet to make its way to La Crosse by 1892, which meant that emergencies like this one required that a person jump onto one of the factory's horses and ride the animal as fast as it could go to find help.

After he had managed to shake loose the horror of what he had seen from his system, the opportunistic thief decided to use his time alone in the building to see if the safe he had seen earlier was as simple to open as he had hoped. To his delight it turned out that it was, which meant that come payday he would be able to get the job done in plenty of time to ensure that he was well away by the time his crime was discovered.

Satisfied that this Wednesday's heist was going to be one of the simplest he had ever undertaken, Porter walked back down to the main floor of the factory and decided that—bloody hanging corpse in the attic or not—he was still hungry and needed to eat something. Luckily, Nils had left behind the lunch his wife had made for him. It was delicious.

He was in the midst of messily devouring an extremely tasty piece of fried chicken when he heard what sounded like footsteps behind him.

"I—" he started, trying to think of a plausible excuse for pilfering his partner's lunch, but when he turned around he saw that he was still alone.

The sound of the footsteps continued. They were heading toward the stairs. Puzzled by what was happening, Porter found himself following them—against his better judgment. As he arrived at the top of the stairs, it was clear that the footsteps were heading toward the dead Mr. Dickens' office, the one with the safe in it. He followed the sound into the room, and there it ended.

"That was—" he started to comment to himself, but he was cut off by the inexplicable sound of a powerful, far-off wind. Frozen in place by his utter confusion, he listened as the sound sped toward him. Suddenly, the door to the room blew shut and the sound stopped. The silence that followed lasted for precisely two seconds. In its place came the chilling echo of a madman's demented cackle. The laughter surrounded him, as if whatever was responsible for it filled the entire room.

Slowly, everything in the room started to shake. Porter ran to the door and tried to open it, but it would not budge. He turned around and his jaw dropped as a pencil on the desk rose up in the air and hurled toward him with the velocity of an arrow. He screamed as it pierced the meaty part of his arm. Then the wooden chair that sat behind the desk slowly slammed with a loud clatter against the door as he jumped out of its way. Papers started flying in the air, moving so fast that their edges sliced into his flesh, inflicting hundreds of painful paper cuts. He tried once again to open the door, but something was keeping it closed. He slammed his body against it, separating his shoulder as he did, but it was far too solid to break down— having been one of the first to be crafted in the very factory in which he was now battling for his life.

He had remained silent throughout this ordeal, but he could not help but scream as he saw the large, heavy safe begin to rise off of the ground. He knew that if it starting flying through the air he would not make it out of the room alive.

He was wrong.

The safe did sail through the air, but he was able to jump out of its way as it—like the chair before it—slammed into the door. The impact proved more than even this well-crafted door could take—it exploded into splinters, some of which flew into Porter, adding further injury to his already bloody and battered body.

Incoherent with pain and fright, he ran screaming out of the room and down the stairs. He was so far gone that he did not see Nils with the town's sheriff and Mr. Pierce. He ran past them and kept on running.

He never returned to La Crosse and he never stole anything ever again.

*   *   *

Poor Mr. Dickens' body was taken down and given a proper burial. To most people his death looked like a suicide, but the lack of a note and the use of barbed wire instead of rope left some convinced that it was something else entirely. But if it was murder, the person who committed the crime was never caught and the question of what really happened to the accountant was never truly answered.

In the weeks that followed the two night watchmen's gruesome discovery, the factory employees felt uneasy coming in to work, complaining that a strange pall had descended upon the building. They were not told much, but the attic where Mr. Dickens was found was locked up tight, and there were rumors that his office had been found in a shambles. Some people even went so far as to say that the safe had been somehow thrown clear through the room's door. If that was true, then a replacement door had to have been put up right away, but it would explain why this new door was now permanently locked.

The events of that night probably would have gone unrecorded and never reached the ears of the factory employees were it not for Jeb, the brother of Pete, one of the lathe operators. Jeb worked as an attendant in a nearby insane asylum and had heard an amazing story from a man who had been sent there for insisting to the authorities that he had been attacked by an angry spirit inside of a local door factory. The terrified man claimed that he had almost been killed when the psychotic ghost hurled a large safe directly at him.

When news of this story hit the factory floor, it allowed the workers there to admit to seeing things they had never told anyone about, lest they too ended up in a straight-jacket. Many of them had heard the eerie sound of laughter; others had felt the breeze of an inexplicable wind; some had actually seen tools and other items floating in the air. These admissions freed the workers from a burden they had all been carrying and gave them the ability to say aloud what many had suspected for quite some time: the factory was haunted by something sinister.

But this suspicion only led to more questions. What was it that was haunting the factory? Why was it there? And did it have anything to do with the death of Mr. Dickens? In the end, these were all questions that would never be answered.

Work continued at the factory, albeit with workers who were now much more vigilant about their safety and sur-roundings. In 1903, George Pierce, the owner of the fac-tory, was found dead in his office. He had last been seen alive by Nils, who observed him at work at his desk late into the night. Although it was officially declared that he had died of a heart attack, many people believed that he was the second man to have been claimed by the factory's mysterious spirit.

Whatever it was that haunted the George Pierce Sash and Door Factory, it proved to be tied to that specific building and not the land it was built on. When the old factory was destroyed and a new one was put up in its place, all reports of haunted activity ceased. But just because the questions of what it was that haunted the old factory or why the ghost was drawn to that building in particular were never answered doesn't mean that different theories haven't been proposed.

According to the first theory, Mr. Dickens, the accountant, really had committed suicide. Unable to live another day crunching numbers that meant nothing to him, he snapped and hanged himself, going so far as to use barbed wire instead of rope to ensure that he would not fail in the pursuit to end his own life. But though death was what he wanted, his spirit remained at the factory, blaming it for driving him to suicide.

And though this would explain why the first major supernatural incident occurred so soon after the accountant's body was found, many doubted his spirit was the true phantom for two reasons. The first reason was that there was evidence that strongly suggested that the building was haunted while he was still alive. The second was that he was universally regarded as a weakling and a sissy who—even in death—would not have had the courage or strength it took to go on otherworldly rampages.

Some people wondered if the spirit belonged to a former employee at the factory who had been laid off when Dickens decided that the numbers proved that the factory could run without him. Despondent over losing his only means of support, this nameless employee committed suicide, and in death returned to the factory to torment the man responsible for him losing his job until Dickens committed suicide as well.

This theory did explain the paranormal occurrences that were observed before Mr. Dickens' death, but it was hampered by the fact that there was no proof that any such employee had existed. No one who worked at the factory could remember ever having heard about someone committing suicide after being fired, especially since no one could remember anyone actually being fired during the time that Dickens worked at the factory.

Those employees who were more conspiratorially minded proposed a theory in which Mr. Pierce had long had a silent partner who owned an equal part of the factory, but who allowed Pierce to make all of the decisions regarding its operation. They suggested that Pierce resented this partner because without him he would be free to enjoy all and not just half of the factory's profits. To that end he hired Dickens, who worked the books so that most of the profit was unrecorded and went directly into Pierce's pockets. This silent partner eventually discovered the scheme and was about to alert the authorities when he was mysteriously killed in an unexplained "accident." Hungry for revenge, the man's spirit haunted the factory and eventually claimed the lives of the two men who cheated him and caused his death.

Despite the popularity of this particular theory, it was easily the most far-fetched and had no discernable connection to reality. There was never any evidence that Mr. Pierce didn't own the factory outright or that Dickens' books were even the slightest bit dishonest. Plus, those who actually knew the two men could not believe that either one of them would be capable of such treachery or duplicity.

In the end, these theories are nothing more than understandable attempts to explain the unexplainable. Many years have passed since the phantom at the old factory last made its presence known, and all the leads that might have led to the truth of its existence have long since vanished. It remains a mystery, one that will likely remain forever unsolved.

Closing Time

Everyone loved old A.J. "Skimmer" Hines. Underneath his crusty German exterior beat a heart that if it wasn't quite gold, had to be at least silver. He had made many a friend during the years he had lived in La Crosse, all of whom knew that his greatest dream in life was to someday open up a saloon just like the ones he remembered back in the old country. It would be a cheery place with a piano to provide music for frequent group sing-a-longs. He would serve the best ales and lagers, along with the tastiest bratwurst in the state. It would be the kind of establishment that good, honest, working folk daydreamed about as they toiled at their daily labors—the kind of place whose existence made hard lives worth living.

Of course, the problem with a dream like this is that it requires a certain amount of capital to make happen—capital that Old Skimmer did not possess. He simply could not afford to build the saloon of his dreams from the ground up. The best he could hope to do would be to buy someone else's saloon and turn it into his own, but for a long time no one was selling. Then, in 1901, he thought he had his chance when Paul Malin, owner of the Malin Pool and Sample Room on 4th Street, dropped dead of a heart attack. Unfortunately, another wannabe saloon owner outbid him for the property and Skimmer's opportunity appeared to vanish. But then a year later, in 1902, the man who had outbid him decided that he no longer wanted to own a tavern and put the property back up for sale. Once again Old Skimmer thought he was on his way to making his dream come true, but history repeated itself and he was forced to lament his fate as another enthusiastic entrepreneur agreed to pay nearly double the original asking price.

Having twice been thwarted, the old man decided to accept that his dream wasn't going to come true, but then—to his astonishment—the property once again went up for sale after only 11 months. But 1903 wasn't his year either; having given up on his dream, he had placed his funds in other investments and couldn't even come up with enough money to meet the minimum asking price, much less the higher amount for which the property eventually sold.

It soon became clear that an odd pattern was forming when the property was put back on the selling block in 1904, but Old Skimmer still couldn't get the money he needed in time. The same was true in 1905, but not in 1906. That year, when the property came up for sale—as if like clockwork—the investments he had made three years earlier finally paid off, and this time he had enough cash to buy it.

Had he not been so obsessed with making his dream come true, he might have stopped and considered what could possibly be so wrong with the property that it had gone on sale each year since its original owner had died, but the thought honestly never occurred to him. And the truth was that, beyond its revolving door of proprietorship, there appeared to be nothing wrong with the saloon. It was always full of people, making a steady profit for all of its owners. Its regular clientele were good, gentle people who caused no trouble. Its foundation was sound and its furnishings were in excellent condition.

If there was a hidden reason for the saloon's constant state of new ownership, the previous owners were not discussing it. Not that Old Skimmer bothered to ask them, but if he had they wouldn't have said a word. They had their reasons for remaining silent.

After two weeks of remodeling, Old Skimmer was able to reopen the saloon—which he named after himself—and the result was everything he had ever dreamed of. In order to help him save money, he converted the back room into a small bedroom, where he slept at night. The saloon was now his home, and he treated everyone who came in like they were special guests.

Along with the regular customers who frequented the place because of its location, most of the many friends he had made during his time in La Crosse also now drank there. The result was a steady stream of income that ensured his investment would prove to be a profitable one.

The first few months were glorious. Pretty waitresses served happy people who sang together or listened with rapt attention as the beaming new proprietor entertained them with one of the long, fanciful stories he was famous for. Although some customers insisted that they had tasted better bratwurst in Milwaukee, Old Skimmer's Saloon was the best place to have a good time in the entire town.

But as more months passed, Old Skimmer's friends and regular customers could not help but notice a change come over their favorite German barkeep. He looked tired and less jovial. He stopped making jokes, and he no longer had the energy to tell his famous stories. He never participated in the group sing-a-longs, and it seemed like a major event when he did something other than pour a beer and yawn. He made the odd decision to buy a pool table, which no one ever used, and then sold it after a few months. Some suggested that the job was simply too much for the old man, but when he hired another bartender so he could take some days off, he did not seem to improve.

Finally a whole year had passed and the old man looked as though he was just days away from crawling into his own grave. He looked miserable as he surprised everyone by ringing the large bell he used to use when he wanted the saloon to be quiet so he could tell a story. This was the first time anyone had heard it in four months.

Everyone stopped talking and turned their attention to the bar. Old Skimmer sighed wearily as he stepped onto the wooden box that used to serve as a stage. As he spoke to them they could tell that it was taking a lot of effort for him to speak loud enough to be heard. "My friends," he said, "I just wanted you to know that I am incredibly grateful for your loyal patronage and the generosity you showed in allowing an old man to live out his dream. But over the past year I have learned that some dreams are best left in your head, where they will always seem perfect and make you happy. I am afraid that I can no longer allow this dream of mine to continue, so—as of tomorrow—I have decided to put my saloon up for sale."

A roar of protest erupted from his staff and customers as all of his friends vocally insisted that he was making a mistake and that there was no reason for him to give up on his lifelong dream after just one year.

"I appreciate your concern," he told them, "but my mind is made up and nothing can be said to dissuade me. I love this place and all of you with all of my heart, but I cannot go on—*I need some sleep!*"

Everyone looked puzzled as they tried to figure out what he meant by this. Operating the bar did entail long hours, but the old man wasn't so overworked that he couldn't rest at night. They waited for him to explain himself, but he didn't say a word. Instead he just stepped off of the box and disappeared into the back room.

It didn't take long for him to find a buyer willing to meet his asking price. Thanks to the steady stream of customers and good location, he was able to make a decent profit on his initial investment—decent enough that he could retire comfortably for the rest of his life. In the months that followed the sale, his health and appearance improved dramatically. Color returned to his cheeks, and the lost twinkle in his eye once again began to sparkle. It was an amazing recovery, all the more so because no one knew what exactly he had recovered from.

For a long time he refused to say anything about his reasons for selling the saloon of his dreams or why he had looked so haggard and tired. Finally, after much goading from his friends, he promised to hold a party at his home, during which he would tell them all the whole story.

That night everyone waited impatiently for Old Skimmer to start telling his story, but he insisted on waiting for everyone to arrive as he served them beer and bratwurst and started a round of group sing-a-longs. When at last everyone who had been invited was there, he sat down in his chair and started telling the story of what had happened to him after he had opened up his saloon.

"As you all must know, I was as excited as any man could be during those first few days of my new adventure," he told them. "I was so wound up by the fun I was having that when the day ended I was often asleep before my head even touched my pillow. Eventually that excitement wore off, and though I very much loved what I was doing, my days were settling into a noticeable routine. This was not a bad thing. I'm old enough to know that a life filled with constant surprises is not always a happy one," he said sagely, "which is why I wasn't happy when such surprises began to awaken me during the middle of the night.

"The first time it happened, the saloon had been open for just over three months. It had been an unusually slow night, mostly because of the poor weather. I had done so little work during the day that I hardly felt the need to go to sleep at my regular time, but I knew that if I did not I would regret it in the morning. As I lay there in my bed, struggling to fall asleep, I instead found my thoughts preoccupied with the many little noises a person hears at night in a quiet building—those little creaks and groans that almost convince your imagination that the structure is alive. I tried to ignore them so I could get some rest, but the longer I lay there the more I heard. After an hour of this I was still wide awake and growing very annoyed with each passing second. It was then that I heard something that shocked me so fiercely that I jumped out of my bed to investigate.

"Although they were quiet, thanks to my closed door and their distance away from me, I heard the distinct sound of footsteps. Now I know that in the silence of the night some sounds can be easily confused with the sound of someone walking, but they are almost always random and without any discernable rhythm. I knew these were real footsteps because they came in the steady beat of a man pacing quickly across a wooden floor. Assuming I had an intruder, I went down on my knees and reached for the shotgun I kept underneath my bed. It wasn't loaded, but I believed that merely presenting it would go a long way toward making my feelings for the intruder clear.

"I opened the door and saw nothing but an impenetrable darkness. I quickly lit a lamp and with it proved to myself that my ears must have been mistaken, because I was the only person to be found. The saloon was completely empty, and the sound of footsteps had ceased. Confused by what had happened, I went back to bed and managed to fall asleep. As strange as the incident was, I saw no need to fret about it the next day and by the time the last customer left for the night I had almost completely forgotten about it. But as I started cleaning up I swore I heard the sound of someone walking around me. Even though I was alone, the sound was unmistakable! Someone was in the room with me, but whoever it was could not be seen!

"My first thought was of a book I had read several years ago by H.G. Wells about a fellow who developed a way to hide himself in plain sight. Then it occurred to me that the most likely source of the footsteps was one that was just as fanciful and equally strange: I was sharing the saloon with a ghost!

"Back in the old country my relatives were forever going on about the spirits that surrounded us. They claimed to have had encounters with phantoms from beyond the grave, but I never believed any of it. It seemed too much like the stuff out of the fairy tales they told us before we went to sleep at night. Still, there was no denying that there was no other earthly phenomenon that could explain what was happening at that moment. As I stood there, I tried to think of what I could do that would prove that I wasn't crazy. How could I get the spirit to do more than just walk noisily around my saloon?

"The only thing I could think of was to speak to it. 'Hey there, noisy,' I said to it, 'what are you so nervous about? The only folks I know who pace like that are busy waiting for their wives to finish giving birth.'

"In the silence that followed I felt like the worst kind of fool. I had once again let my imagination get the better of me, or so I thought. My fears of my potential lunacy were ended when I saw the hazy spirit of a man form right in front of my eyes, and though I am well aware that some would see this as an excuse to doubt their sanity, I did not. I knew that what I was seeing was not a hallucination or an idle fantasy; it was the real thing.

"And as my mind reeled from the enormity of what I was seeing, it was further shocked by what happened next. The spirit, not content to merely be seen, began to speak. 'Hey there, pal,' the phantom said to me, 'can't you see I'm dying here for a game of pool?'

"With this question I knew at once whose spirit was standing in front of me. It was Paul Malin, the original owner of the building when it had housed a pool hall. Although I did not know it at the time, I eventually discovered that his spirit was distressed that the man who had purchased the property following his death had sold off all of his beloved pool tables, believing them to be magnets for a disreputable crowd. During the years that followed, Malin's spirit did everything it could to let the current owners of the property know that it was unhappy with the current state of affairs, and its nocturnal antics drove them all to sell their businesses within a year.

"I must admit that I thought I was made of sterner stuff than my predecessors. As the days progressed and I learned the truth behind the spirit's dissatisfaction, I figured I could easily appease it by purchasing a pool table, which I would place in the dark, far-off corner that usually went unused on even the busiest of nights. What I hadn't counted on was how damn loud Malin's ghost would be once he had a pool table to play with. All night long all I heard was the clattering of billiard balls as his spirit played game after game.

"One night it got so bad that I got out of bed to have a word with my phantom guest. 'I have a business to run,' I told him, 'and I need my rest, which I can't get while I have to listen to you making that infernal racket each and every night.'

"For the most part, Malin's spirit preferred to stay unseen, but on this occasion he appeared before me, and though his features remained hazy, I could tell that he had a wicked grin on his face. 'Are you a wagering man?' he asked me.

"'I've made a bet or two in my day,' I told him.

"'Well then,' he continued, 'how about we solve our problem with a little sportsmanship? Each night we'll play a game of Nine Ball. If you win, I won't touch the pool table for the rest of the night; but if I win, I can play until the break of dawn. Deal?'

"'All right,' I agreed, believing that this was a more than fair way to solve our dilemma—especially because back in my younger days I had spent a fair amount of time in various pool halls around the world, and Nine Ball had always been my game of choice. I suspected that Malin's spirit thought I would be an easy mark to hustle, but he would soon learn otherwise.

"For those of you that are unfamiliar with the game, its basic rules are quite simple. There are ten balls on the table, including the white cue ball and nine colored balls marked one through nine. With each shot the player is obligated to hit the lowest-numbered ball still on the table, but he doesn't necessarily have to sink that ball. If he is able to pot a higher ball by hitting it with the lower ball, then that counts as a successful cue. And because the object of the game is to be the fellow who pots the nine ball, it is possible to win with your very first shot, as long as you can sink the nine ball after first connecting with the one ball. There are also various arcane rules that make the game slightly more difficult than it sounds. They tend to only be observed by the sort of fellows who have discovered that it is just as easy to cheat by obsessively following the rules as it is to ignore them.

"'I made the wager,' said Malin's spirit, 'so you get to break.'

"I nodded silently and picked up one of the cues propped up in the corner. It wasn't as straight as I would have liked, but then that was my fault for being so cheap when I bought them in the first place. And though I was once quite adept at the game, it had been at least 20 years since I last played it and I worried that I might have forgotten everything I had once known about it.

"It turned out that my fears were unwarranted, because with my break I was able to use the one ball to sink the seven. This allowed me to continue, and I sank the one. With my next shot I managed to hit the two but did not sink any balls, which meant it was now the ghost's turn to play.

"Before I tell you what he did, I'd like to take a moment to say that many of my very favorite moments in life happened when my expectations proved to be wrong. A life without surprises is one that isn't worth living, as far as I'm concerned. I tell you this because I was expecting Malin to go on to clear the table without giving me another chance to make a shot. How could I not? The fellow used to own a pool hall, and he died playing the game we were engaged in right at that moment. Plus, he had spent hours each night for the past month playing the game over and over again, so what else could I assume but my own quick defeat?

"But what I immediately learned at that moment was that passion for a game does not necessarily translate into skill. Despite his many hours spent at a pool table throughout both his life and death, Malin simply wasn't very good. He certainly tried his best, but his touch was poor and his choices nearly always wrong. With his first shot he missed the two ball by a wide margin. This was a foul, which allowed me to take the ball in hand, which just means that for my next shot I could pick up the cue ball and place it wherever I thought it would be to my best advantage. As I held the white ball and looked to see how I should play it, I saw that there was a way for me to sink the nine using the two. It was a hard shot, but well worth the risk, so I decided to take it. I placed the cue ball on the table and made sure that the geometry in my head was correct. When I was certain that it was, I bent over and took my shot. Much to my delight, the nine ball went into the left side pocket and I had won the game.

"'Good game,' I said to the spirit, 'now if you don't mind, I would like to get some sleep.' And though I could tell that the ghost was not at all pleased with my victory, it stayed true to its word and did not play another game for the rest of the night, leaving me to get the rest I needed in peace.

"After that, in the month that followed, I had to add another chore to my closing duties. After I had put up the chairs and swept the floor, I had to play a game of Nine Ball with Malin's spirit. I'd like to say that I won every one of these matches, but no one is perfect, and there were some nights that the ghost was able to capitalize on one of my mistakes and earn the right to play by himself until dawn. But that only happened a handful of times. Most nights the ghost had to be content with just the one game, and as time went on I could tell that it was not happy with this arrangement.

"The breaking point came during a match in which the ghost was having one of those rare moments when a bad or mediocre player suddenly finds himself unable to do anything wrong. As the winner of the previous game it was up to me to decide who broke, and for a change of pace I allowed my competitor to start the game. This wasn't really an act of generosity on my part because I was certain I would soon have a chance at the table.

"My confidence soon wavered, however, as the ghost proceeded to pull off a series of increasingly difficult shots. Within 10 minutes he was in a position to win the game, with just the nine ball remaining on the table. If you had asked me when I was younger if I would ever be in the position to see a spirit from the afterlife smile with a grin of smug satisfaction, I would have laughed in your face, but there I was watching it happen.

"'Get ready to stay up all night, old man,' the ghost said somewhat arrogantly, 'because this shot is going to win me the game.'

"I couldn't help but frown as I stood there and waited for him to claim his victory. I've never had any use for a poor sport, even ones from beyond the grave. But my displeasure soon transformed into happiness when Malin's spirit proceeded to miss the easiest shot he had faced during the entire game.

"'Blast it!' he roared, throwing down his cue on the floor with the kind of anger that only comes when a person has failed to capitalize on a sure thing. I didn't even bother hiding my smile as I then bent over and quickly potted the nine ball in a corner pocket to win the game.

"It is moments like these that make you realize what a cruel game Nine Ball really is. The spirit of Paul Malin had played the best game of his life only to have me win it with a single shot. Such a humiliation, piled on top of so many others, was too much for the ghost to bear. With a cry of anger, the likes of which I had never heard before, the phantom vanished right before my eyes. Such was the vehemence of his exit that I actually believed that this might be the last time I would ever see the spirit. Unfortunately, I was wrong.

"That night I was awoken by a banging and a pounding that made me wonder if we were in the midst of an earthquake. I got out of bed, and though my room was not shaking, the noise continued. I lit a lamp and went out into the saloon, and there I saw Malin's ghost creating the loudest ruckus he possibly could with the materials available to him.

"'Hey!' I shouted at the spirit. 'I thought you were an honorable ghost,' I chided him, 'yet here you are breaking the terms of our wager just because you are a poor loser.'

"'I'm doing nothing of the sort!' the spirit told me. 'Our wager clearly stated that if I lost I would not be able to play pool for the rest of the night, and I have not once touched the pool table since we last played.'

"He had me. There was nothing in our agreement to stop him from making as loud a racket as he wanted, as long as he did not play any pool. I went back to bed but did not get any sleep. The next night I told the spirit that I wanted to change the particulars of our wager, so that if he lost he would have to be completely silent for the entire night.

"'I do not find that term to be acceptable,' the spirit told me. 'I will not agree to it.'

"'Very well,' I answered back, 'then I shall play with you no more, and tomorrow the pool table will be taken away.'

"In all my time with the phantom, I had never once had any cause to be frightened. That changed when I saw the look of hatred on the spirit's face. 'You do that,' it threatened me, 'and you will regret it.'

"Those of you who know me well know that I am not a man who reacts well to threats like this. The next morning—which took forever to come thanks to the spirit's noisy protests—I sold the pool table and had it taken away.

"After that there was no calming the spirit down. Each night it made as much noise as it possibly could, until finally I was becoming ill from the lack of sleep. I know you were all so concerned about my well-being during that time, and you were upset because I refused to tell you what was wrong, but how could I? You would have thought I was mad! I suppose many of you think I am mad right now, but enough time has passed for me to be certain enough of my own sanity that I do not care. Besides, I am not the first person to tell such stories here in La Crosse. I'm sure many of you have heard the tales of the spirit that is said to haunt the late George Pierce's door factory.

"Finally it became too much for me to bear. I had no choice but to sell my saloon or drop dead from exhaustion, and as much as I loved the place, it was not worth ending my life for." Old Skimmer smiled and took a long sip from his beer.

"Now then," he said after his thirst had been quenched, "let me tell you a much more interesting story about the talking mouse I discovered when I was…"

As word spread of Old Skimmer's explanation for why the saloon on 4th Street never stayed in one man's possession for more than a year, people asked the other former owners if there was any truth to it. None of them would confirm or deny the story the old German had told. Eventually the bar was sold to a man who managed to hold onto it for longer than a year. It is not known if he was able to do this because he did not live in the saloon, like the others had, or because the spirit that had caused so much trouble had finally gone away.

The Keepsake

Teddy King was nearly out the door on his way to work when his ears were pierced by his wife Ethel's irritatingly nasal voice.

"Teddy," she nagged at him in that shrill way she had adopted the day after they were married, "don't forget that you have to dig up your mother today."

"I won't, dear," he sighed, certain that were it not for that one extra piece of bacon he had eaten, he would have gotten out of the house in time to avoid this conversation.

"You've been saying that for over a month now! Today's the last day to get it done, so you better get out to the cemetery as soon as you get off work."

"I will, dear," he promised her.

"You better!"

*   *   *

At the tail end of July 1936, everyone in St. Croix County who had a relative buried in Knapp Cemetery received a letter from the local officials informing them that a road had been commissioned to be built in the path of the graveyard. They were further informed that because of this development, they were left with two options—move their ancestor's body to another location or accept the fact that automobiles were going to be driving over the remains of their dear ones.

Although a few unkind souls did choose to take the latter of these two options, most people were conscientious enough to take steps to ensure that their relatives' remains were moved to more peaceful pastures. Many of these folks paid others to do this dirty work for them, but some—like Teddy—could not afford such an extravagance and were forced to take on the job themselves.

A procrastinator by nature, Teddy had waited until the very last day before construction of the road was to begin. He had asked several of his buddies to help him out, but none of them considered him a good enough friend to aid him in this particular activity. He was going to have to do it all by himself.

The sun was already setting as he left work to go to the cemetery. It started to gradually dawn on him what he was about to do. He briefly considered that it might be for the best to leave his mother where she was. She had never been a timid woman, and she might even like the hustle and bustle of being buried underneath a popular roadway. He dismissed this thought when it occurred to him that if he returned home without his mother's body (as he had yet to find another place to put it), Ethel would never let him hear the end of it.

Teddy wasn't a smart man, but he knew one thing for sure—he vastly preferred the possible dangers inherent in digging up a grave at night to the certain dangers that went hand in hand with displeasing his wife. The world's scariest spook was no match for Ethel when she was angry.

By the time he drove through the cemetery gates, the sky was completely dark and the various local creatures of the night were all coming out to sing their nocturnal songs. This atmosphere did little to soothe Teddy's fraying nerves, but he continued along anyway and got out of his car, picked up his shovel and a small kerosene lamp and headed for his mother's grave.

As he made his way through the cemetery, he was slightly unnerved by the sight of hundreds of open graves, each one a reminder of what they had once contained. He tried his best to ignore them, but he kept flashing back to a story he had once read in a pulp magazine about what happened when all of the tenants of a quiet graveyard decided they wanted a change of pace and started crawling out of the ground.

This thought was enough to cause perspiration to bead on his forehead. He wiped it away with a handkerchief and wondered if it was a bad sign that he was sweating before he had even had a chance to put his shovel into the ground.

With a grateful sigh he finally reached his mother's grave, which was marked by a small headstone. Not wanting to have to pay for a new marker in the future, he dug up this old one so it could be reused wherever they eventually decided to put her. He then started digging up the grave in earnest. It was hard work and his arms were starting to ache before he was even a quarter of the way finished. Each shovel-full of dirt started getting heavier and heavier, and with each one he cursed his friends for not being willing to help him out. He would definitely remember this the next time any one of them ever asked him for a favor.

"Hey, Mr. King, what are you doing?"

The question came so suddenly and unexpectedly that Teddy literally jumped in the air when he heard it. His heart raced as he turned around and saw a familiar face standing behind him. It was Lloyd Owens, the young man who had been working at the nearby Larson farm since the start of summer.

"You scared me, Lloyd," Teddy told him breathlessly. "The last thing a fellow wants to hear when he's alone in a graveyard is someone else's voice."

"I'm sorry, Mr. King," Lloyd apologized. "I didn't mean no harm. I was just about to go to bed when I looked out my window and saw you out here all alone. I wondered about what you were up to, so I thought I'd come out and see. I'm guessing now that you're moving a relative like all of the other folks have been doing this month."

"That's right," Teddy nodded. "This is my mother's grave."

"Sure is an awfully big job for someone to do all by himself," sympathized Lloyd. "Could you use some help?"

"I can't afford to pay you anything, Lloyd," Teddy answered honestly.

"Don't worry about that, Mr. King," said Lloyd. "Sometimes a fellow does these sort of things because it's his Christian duty, not because he expects a few dollars in return."

"If that's the case," said Teddy, "I would definitely appreciate any help you could give me."

"I'll just go and grab another shovel from the farm," said Lloyd. He then disappeared for a few minutes before he returned with a shovel in his hands.

With Lloyd's help, Teddy was able to dig his mother out of her penultimate resting place in a third of the time it would have taken him if he had been left to work alone. Getting the coffin out of the hole proved to be a bit more difficult than he had counted on, but Lloyd borrowed some ropes from the farm and they managed to have her out of there and loaded onto Teddy's car in just over an hour.

"Thanks for the help, Lloyd," Teddy said gratefully as he packed up his stuff and prepared to head home with his dead mother.

"Always glad to oblige, Mr. King," Lloyd smiled back.

Teddy then sighed at the thought of returning to his wife and got into his car and drove away. Lloyd waved to him as he drove off and then turned to pick up the ropes and shovel he had taken from the farm. As he grabbed them he noticed something shiny lying on the ground. He picked it up and saw that it was a silver handle that must have fallen off Mrs. King's casket.

At first Lloyd thought he'd hold onto it so he could return it to Teddy the next time he saw him in town, but then—as he looked at it reflecting the moonlight—he decided it might make for an interesting souvenir. How many folks could say that they owned a genuine silver handle from a coffin that had been buried in the ground for over 10 years? None that he knew of, and so, with that settled, he stuck the handle in his pocket and returned to the farm.

It was getting late, and Lloyd decided it was time to go to bed. He took the handle out of his pocket and put it on top of his dresser, then got undressed and climbed onto his bed. Normally he had no need for blankets at this time of year; the warm summer air made them superfluous. But as he lay there he felt an unusual chill creep across the room, so he pulled a sheet on top of himself and—when that proved to be not enough to fight the cold—he pulled up the heavy quilt that normally saw use only in the winter months. This managed to warm him up enough so that he was comfortable and able to fall asleep. But just a few hours later his slumber was interrupted when he felt the same chill from before creeping all over his body. He opened his eyes and noticed with sleepy surprise that both the sheet and the quilt were now lying on the floor.

"Must have kicked them off in my sleep," he whispered to himself as he pulled them back onto his cold body. With them back in place he was able to sleep comfortably for another hour, after which he awoke again to the bite of the room's unexplainable chill. "I must have restless legs tonight," he muttered to himself as he looked and saw that his blankets were once again lying on the floor. He pulled them back on his body and once more fell asleep.

This time Lloyd was able to sleep undisturbed until it was time for him to wake up. Groggy and annoyed to have had—what was for him—a very restless night's sleep, he got out of bed and got dressed. As he slipped into his overalls, he looked down and noticed something glimmering on the floor. It was the coffin handle, which he could have sworn he left on top of his dresser.

"There must be a draft in here I don't know about," he told himself, as that was the only way he could think of to explain both last night's chill and finding the silver handle on the floor. Vowing to find the source of the draft the next time he got a free moment, he placed the silver handle back on top of his dresser and left to do his morning chores.

But it didn't take Lloyd long to forget his vow as his thoughts turned to the work of the day. By the time he returned to his room it was time for him to clean up before dinner, and he had forgotten all about the mysterious draft. As he walked into his room he noticed something twinkling on the floor. He bent over to pick it up and saw it that was the coffin handle he had found the night before.

"You just don't want to stay up on that dresser, do you?" Lloyd spoke to it as he looked at it in his hand. "I better just keep you in my pocket until I find the breeze that keeps blowing you onto the floor."

"Who are you talking to?" asked a voice from outside his bedroom door. It was Mrs. Larson.

"No one," Lloyd admitted, embarrassed to be caught talking to himself like that.

"Dinner's ready," she told him. "Come and get it before it gets cold."

"Yes, ma'am," Lloyd nodded his head as he slipped the silver handle into his pocket.

Mrs. Larson was a very good cook and Lloyd was a man with a very large appetite, so a full hour passed before he returned to his room. When he did, he saw something that made his jaw drop: there on the floor was the silver handle from Mrs. King's casket.

Lloyd reached into his pocket and discovered that it was empty. Assuming that it must have a hole in it, he pulled it out to inspect it and discovered that it was completely intact. "Well, I'll be a son of a gun," he shook his head. "It's not a draft, is it? You really want to get my attention, don't you?"

"Who are you talking to?" he heard a familiar voice ask behind him.

Lloyd turned around and saw that he had once again been caught talking to himself by Mrs. Larson. "Just to myself, Mrs. Larson," he answered honestly.

"You're not going crazy on us, are you, Lloyd?" she asked him.

"No, ma'am. I don't think so, but then I guess if I was I wouldn't be the best person to judge, would I?"

"I suppose," she agreed before changing the subject. "Henry wanted me to ask you to go help him with Mary. It looks like she's about to birth her first colt."

"I'll be right there," he told her.

She hesitated at his doorway for a moment with a concerned expression on her face, as if she wondered if it was wise to leave him alone with himself, before she finally turned away and headed back to the kitchen.

Lloyd closed his door so he would not be interrupted again and pulled out the shoebox he kept underneath his bed. This box was where he kept his money and other assorted small treasures and mementos he had held on to over the years. He always kept it tied up with string as an added security measure, which included a secret knot he was certain only he knew how to undo. He undid the knot, took off the lid and dropped the silver handle into the box. He then replaced the lid, retied the knot and slipped the box back underneath his bed. With that done, he opened his door and went out to the barn to help Mr. Larson with Mary's birth.

It was quite late when Lloyd got back to his room, and he was so tired he couldn't even be bothered to take off his clothes as he fell onto his bed, which was why he didn't notice that the strange chill from last night had returned once again. This time he slept without interruption all the way until it was time for him to get up. It was only then, as he rose sleepily out of his bed, that he was jolted instantly awake. There was the silver coffin handle lying on his floor, free from the bonds of his shoebox, which—when he examined it—remained in exactly the same state as he had left it.

It was official. Lloyd was now completely spooked.

He picked up the handle and tried to think of his options. He obviously couldn't keep it like he had planned, which meant that he had to get rid of it. He could give it back to Teddy King, but he didn't know when he would next run into Teddy, and he didn't have the transportation required to travel to Teddy's home—at least not today, and he really want to get rid of the haunted souvenir as soon as possible. Lloyd was left with only one option he could think of.

With the handle still in his hand he ran out of his room and out of the house. Once he got outside he kept on running until he reached Knapp Cemetery, which was—at that very moment—being turned into a new roadway. The crew doing the work had yet to reach the part of the cemetery where Mrs. King had been buried, so her empty grave was still as he and Teddy had left it. Whispering a quick prayer he dropped the silver coffin handle into the grave and hoped that this would be the last time he ever saw it.

His hope was fulfilled, and for the rest of his life Lloyd Owens avoided collecting any unusual souvenirs.

Shallow Water

Whenever Jack wanted to visit his girlfriend, Tammy, he had to walk the five miles that lay between the small farm he worked at and the even smaller town of Menomenie, where she lived. Luckily for him, he seldom had to make this trip alone, since his friend Franklin, who worked at the next farm next over, was dating Tammy's sister Taffy and was therefore required to make the journey as often as he was.

Neither was prone to any sort of philosophizing—in fact, neither had education enough to know what philosophizing was—so the talk was mainly about their girlfriends. That was why one night in particular was so different from the rest, as their regular discussion had somehow inexplicably evolved into a debate about the particulars and possibilities of life after death.

Both of them were good Christian boys who believed that the human spirit continued after the body died off, but they did not see eye to eye on what could happen to that spirit after the body was gone. Jack was adamant that a person's spirit went straight to either heaven or hell, depending on how that person had lived his or her life, and that was that. Franklin agreed that that was what happened to most peoples' spirits, but he also believed that some folks were given the choice of a third option, which allowed them to stay among the living and remain as a ghostly fragment of what they used to be.

"That's hooey," Jack insisted. "There ain't no such thing as ghosts. Why would a person who could go to heaven choose to remain here, when paradise is only a few steps away? And why should we fear going to hell if we can avoid it by staying here?"

"Because for some people," Franklin answered him, "paradise don't mean that much if it means being away from their loved ones or leaving something that's important to them behind. And just because a spirit stays on the Earth for a while, doesn't mean it can avoid its eventual fate. If a spirit is supposed to go to hell, it will eventually— just later than expected."

"No way, no how," Jack shook his head in disagreement. "You're saying that people have a choice over what we do when we die and we don't—we either go straight to heaven or straight to hell and that's it. God doesn't give us any other options."

"What about Limbo and Purgatory?"

"What-bo and where's-it?"

"According to the Catholics, those are other places people's souls can go to besides the two main locations. Limbo is for the souls of babies who died before they could be baptized and Purgatory is for folks who did wrong, but not enough to go to hell. They stay there for a set amount of years and then get to go to heaven."

"Don't sound right to me," said Jack. "How do you know so much about it anyway?"

"Dory told me all about it," Franklin answered, referring to a fellow farmhand. "He's a Catholic. They sure have some interesting beliefs."

"They can believe whatever they want—I know what I learned at Sunday school and I see no reason to change my mind now."

Knowing that his friend wasn't capable of engaging in this discussion with an open mind, Franklin decided to change the subject back to a discussion about their girl-friends. That was when they noticed a figure walking toward them in the distance.

It was a woman, young and fragile looking, dressed in a long white slip that did little to protect her skin from the cold night air. Her hair was long and dark, styled similarly to the way Tammy kept hers.

"Is that your girlfriend?" asked Franklin.

It was a valid question. Taffy and Tammy were the only two women in Menomenie who even came close to looking like the young woman on the road, but she was still too far away for them to identify her for sure.

"Hey Tammy!" Jack shouted out. "What are you doing walking outside dressed like that? You'll catch a cold before you even know it!"

The woman did not respond.

"I don't think it's Tammy," Franklin decided.

"Sure it is," said Jack. "Who else could it be? She must have not heard me, that's all."

It was hard for Franklin to disagree. Menomenie was such a small town that anyone who was there for a week got to know everyone who lived there and in the surrounding area, so the chances of coming across someone they didn't recognize were almost nonexistent. Sometimes they saw someone pass by on a horse, in a buggy or even in one of those fancy new motorcars on their way to somewhere else, but he couldn't think of a single time he came across a stranger walking down the road. Especially one dressed like the woman walking toward them now.

"Tammy!" Jack shouted again.

Once again the woman ignored him, and when she was almost close enough to identify for certain, she turned to the right and walked off of the road toward the shallow stream that ran along the area.

"Tammy!" Jack tried one last time. "What are you doing?"

Determined to find out what was happening, the two men started running toward the woman, who had reached the stream and was about to step into it. As they ran, they saw her walk into the shallow water, which would have been nearly ice cold this time of year.

"Are you crazy, girl?" Jack shouted at her, but she did not seem to hear him.

By the time they reached the stream, she was halfway across it. The two of them shouted at her, trying to get her to turn around, but she ignored them. And then, just before she reached the other side of the stream, she did something that neither Jack nor Franklin would have expected to see in a million years.

She vanished.

A full minute passed before the two stunned young men could say anything about what they just saw.

"Did she—" asked Jack.

"Yes," answered Franklin.

"She was—"

"—and then she wasn't."

"Right in—"

"—front of our eyes."

Still unsure of what they had actually seen, the two men ran into the icy water toward the spot where the woman had disappeared. Although they did not believe it, they wanted to be sure that she hadn't fallen down a hidden hole in the stream. She hadn't.

When Tammy and Taffy opened their front door they found their boyfriends shivering on their doorstep, both of them as pale as bed sheets.

The two young women had spent much of their lives playing in the stream in which the mysterious girl had disappeared, so they knew that there were no dangerous spots where a person could suddenly be sucked under the water. If the girl had vanished like their boyfriends had said she did, then there had to be another explanation for it.

Jack and Franklin never did find out who the woman was or why they had seen her that night, but for the rest of his life Jack was much more open to the concept of ghosts.

3
Haunted Women

Victoria's Jailhouse Experience

Victoria hadn't meant to murder her husband—it just worked out that way. No one would believe her that it was an accident, that she hadn't deliberately mixed rat poison in his biscuits—and who could blame them? Charlie Anderson was a person many people wanted to see dead, including many members of his own family, so it surprised no one when his own wife finally got around to doing what everyone else had merely dreamed of.

Charlie had been one of those people who is very easy to hate, even though he never actually did anything that a fair person would describe as wicked or evil. He had not been an abusive man, and could never have been accused of being belligerent. He had never treated anyone dishonestly and he had always been careful to pay back all of his debts, yet he remained almost universally loathed by everyone who had ever spent time with him.

There were two reasons for this loathing. The first reason was that he was cursed with an affliction that seemingly left him unable to let any one of his thoughts go unexpressed. Being around him meant being barraged by an endless stream of pointless comments and meaningless observations. It only took a few minutes for a complete stranger to become exhausted by his inexhaustible chatter, so one can only imagine the suffering it caused among those who had known him his entire life.

The second reason that everyone hated him served as proof that there is nothing the universe loves more than a good dose of irony to sweeten the absurdity of any situation. In this case, it was that in those ultra-rare moments when Charlie was mute, one became acutely aware of a permanent blockage in his nasal cavity that caused his nose to whistle whenever he exhaled, thus ensuring that even when he had stopped talking, he was incapable of being silent.

One may fairly wonder why Victoria would marry a man as endlessly irritating as Charlie, but she had a good excuse. She had been a mail-order bride and had never met him until the day of their marriage, which was on the same day she arrived in Madison after a long trip from her hometown of Albany, New York. The date was August 5, 1872, exactly a year to the day before Charlie was found dead at his kitchen table.

Following the local doctor's determination that Charlie had indeed been poisoned and further determination that the poison could be found in the biscuits that had been found sitting on his plate, Victoria was arrested and held for trial at the Madison Jailhouse.

The common sentiment among those familiar with Victoria's situation was that she had shown remarkable strength lasting as long as she did before she finally snapped and decided to silence Charlie for good. Still, as understandable as her crime may have been, it was still a crime, and Victoria had to be held accountable for her actions no matter how much she denied deliberately adding the poison into the biscuit batter.

Unused to having female prisoners at the jailhouse, her keepers did their best to make sure she was comfortable and kept away from the male prisoners, who were—as a group—not famed for their good manners or decorum.

One would like to think that Victoria received this special treatment owing to the natural kindness of the men who ran the jail. But no, it is very easy to suspect that a great deal of the special attention she earned from her keepers was because she was the kind of woman whose features brought pleasure to those lucky enough to be exposed to them. In short, she was a looker with the kind of figure that turned grown men into wide-eyed little boys.

Why, if she was truly this attractive, could she not have found a man in Albany, rather than get married to a stranger in Wisconsin? Victoria was actually a better match for Charlie than one would first presume. For though she possessed an attractive face and body, she had been cursed with a voice so high-pitched and naturally whiny that every time she spoke, all dogs within a 10-mile radius were driven to thoughts of suicide. Knowing how she sounded, she spoke very rarely. All of the men who attempted to court her in her hometown mistook her silence for indifference and soon gave up on her, and so she chose to become a mail-order bride believing that was the only way she would ever get married. She was not lying when she claimed that Charlie's death was an accident; she was the one person who truly appreciated his constant chatter because it spared her the humiliation of ever having to speak for herself.

Her attempts to explain what had really happened had thus far failed to convince the authorities. Too embarrassed by her voice to express herself vocally, she tried giving her version of events by writing them down on paper. Unfortunately, her education had been very limited owing to her father's belief that going to school only gave a person ideas, and ideas were the reason the whole world was going to hell in a handbasket, so she lacked the ability to properly get her story across. And, having long mastered the ability to say specific words like "yes," "no" and "hello" in a pretend voice she had never been able to employ for complete sentences, everyone knew she wasn't a mute and so assumed that her reluctance to speak was a sure sign of her guilt.

Perhaps most people would forget their pride when faced with the threat of the hangman's noose, but Victoria was not one of them. If she had chosen to fully communicate the cause of Charlie's death, the following is what she would have told them: "We had been having a problem with rats, so Charlie had gone out to buy some poison because the traps we had set out to catch them just weren't working. The only kind that the local grocer had on hand was a brand—whose name I can't recall for reasons you'll soon appreciate—that came in a container similar to the kind used by the folks who manufacture the brand of flour I prefer. The problem was that it was raining that day and as Charlie walked home, the canister of poison got wet and its label peeled right off. I noticed this when he handed the canister to me. I made a note not to put it anywhere near the flour because their containers did look so similar, especially since by an unfortunate coincidence the flour's label had also peeled off a few days earlier.

"But I'm afraid I forgot, because Charlie distracted me with a blow-by-blow account of everything he saw and encountered on his way to and from the grocer's. My husband had a way of stretching a conversation past points most people would take them, and by the time he left me to take care of a repair he needed to attend to, I had forgotten about the necessity of keeping the rat poison away from the flour. In fact I had completely forgotten what I had done with the canister after Charlie had handed it to me and started talking.

"I thought nothing of it as I started to prepare our dinner, which was going to be mostly leftovers from the night before. I just had to make some buttermilk biscuits, which Charlie loved, and from there I think you can guess what happened next. When I went to get the ingredients I needed for the biscuits I saw what I thought was the flour canister on top of the kitchen counter and I used the white powder it contained to make the biscuits. Working with the dough I found myself becoming light-headed, but it never occurred to me that it was because I was working with poison instead of flour. By the time I put the biscuits into the oven to bake I was so light-headed that I felt I was about to pass out. I told Charlie that I was feeling sick and he told me to lie down and that he would finish my work in the kitchen and eat while I rested. I was in bed for an hour when it suddenly occurred to me why I was feeling so ill and—realizing what I had done—I jumped out of the bed and ran to our dining room and discovered that I was too late. Charlie had eaten one of the rat poison biscuits and had died. So you see, don't you? This wasn't murder, but a horrible, horrible accident!"

A quick investigation would have easily backed up her story and at least resulted in a lesser punishment than the noose she was facing, if not her outright freedom. But Victoria's pride was greater than her fear of death, so she remained silent and awaited the trial that would decide her fate.

*　　　*　　　*

It wasn't so bad in jail. Her guards were very kind to her, and she wasn't forced to share a cell with anyone else. She spent her time knitting a sweater she intended to wear at the trial. The food wasn't pleasant and it got drafty at night, but beyond that she had had worst experiences in her life—until she started hearing the screams of her fellow prisoners.

The first time Victoria heard the screaming she thought it was a part of the dream she was having. Up to that point her dream had been a pleasant fantasy involving her being taught how to ride a horse by a handsome young cavalry officer, but then, just as he was about to tenderly caress her hair, he stopped short and started shrieking like a maniac. It took her a moment to realize that the source of this sound was coming from outside her own mind and another moment before she was able to open her eyes. All she saw was the same familiar darkness she had grown used to during the week of nights she had spent in the jail, but her ears heard something she had yet to experience in her time there—the sound of genuine terror.

"GET IT OUT OF ME!" she heard a voice shout in the darkness. "I CAN FEEL IT IN MY SOUL!" This declaration was followed by a scream of such terrible agony that she could not bear to listen to it. She held her hands over her ears, but the sound of the poor man's horror could not be blocked out.

She sat up in her cot and watched as a guard ran by her cell with an oil lamp in his hand. "You be quiet, Johnson!" the guard yelled at the screaming prisoner, trying to control the situation, but it was clear from the waver in his voice that he was just as spooked by the man's cries as Victoria was.

"IT'S IN MY SOUL! I CAN FEEL IT! GET IT OUT OF ME! GET IT OUT!" the man continued to shout.

"Johnson, I swear—" the guard attempted to think of a threat that would get the terrified prisoner to stop screaming, but before one came to him the man was silent.

The resulting quiet was interrupted only by the sound of the prisoner's body falling to the floor.

"He's dead," Vicoria heard the guard say to no one in particular. "He just keeled over and dropped dead."

She did not get any more sleep that night.

*   *   *

The next day there was a buzz in the jailhouse as the prisoners and the guards whispered the news of the previous night's strange disturbance back and forth between themselves. Johnson had apparently had a heart attack caused by the stress of his terror. Victoria was the only one who had nothing to say about his bizarre death, but that had more to do with her shame regarding her voice than it did a lack of interest or concern.

"He kept saying that something was in his soul," she heard a guard say to another guard as they stood outside her cell, "but Gavin didn't see anything in there with him."

"Ah, the fellow was just a loony," said the other guard. "He was in here for vagrancy and you know how those bums are—they're lucky if they happen to know their own name."

"I suppose," shrugged the other guard, "but what do you think he was imagining that could have scared him so badly it killed him?"

"How should I know? I'm not a loony. That's the good thing about having all of your wits about you—you don't have to understand what goes on in the heads of maniacs."

The two men walked off, leaving Victoria alone to ponder the question the second guard was unwilling to consider—what could possibly frighten a man so much it killed him where he stood?

She couldn't think of an answer.

*   *   *

The air in the jailhouse was a solid mass of anticipation as the day ended and it became time for the prisoners to lay in their cots for the night. Would another prisoner be visited by the entity that Johnson claimed had entered his soul, or had that all been nothing more than the delusional fantasy of a crazy old vagrant? None of them were able to sleep as they waited for the answer.

For Victoria the tension was unbearable, and the time passed as though the universe had been dipped in amber and slowed to an eternal standstill. It got to the point that she would have welcomed the sounds of another person's screams just so she could get some sleep afterward. None came.

After what seemed like a year, the light of dawn began to glimmer through her cell's tiny window to the outside world. The next day had arrived and no one's soul had been invaded. Johnson had been just a crazy old coot after all.

That night the atmosphere in the jailhouse was much more relaxed, with all of the guards and prisoners now certain that they had nothing to be afraid of. Exhausted from their lack of sleep the previous night, the prisoners easily drifted off into dreamland, where they were free to do whatever they pleased.

As had become her habit, Victoria dreamed of her cavalry officer and the horse he was so patiently teaching her how to ride, although this time the focus was much more on the man than the animal. He and Victoria were having a picnic in a beautiful green field as the sun started to set in the distance. The officer was in the process of leaning forward to kiss her when he suddenly stopped and—just as he had the last time he attempted an intimacy in one of her dreams—he started to scream.

She awoke immediately and sat up on her cot. The screams were coming from both of the men in the cell right next to hers. Separated by concrete walls rather than bars, she had never seen the men who were imprisoned next to her, but she was very familiar with their voices, so she could definitely hear how frightened they truly were.

"SOMETHING FLEW INTO MANNY!" she heard one of them shout to the guard on duty, who was running toward their cell. "Something unholy has possessed his body!"

"GET IT OUT OF ME!" Manny screamed. "GET IT OUT! I CAN FEEL IT IN ME!" Victoria shuddered when she realized what he was going to say next. "IT'S IN MY SOUL!" he cried. "I CAN FEEL IT IN MY SOUL!"

The guard opened up the cell and ordered the other prisoner to sit on the floor.

"I want out of here!" the prisoner insisted.

"Sit down!" the guard ordered again.

"I want out!"

Victoria listened as a struggle between the two men ensued. It ended with the sound of the prisoner's body hitting the floor after receiving a sharp blow to the head from the guard's club. All the while Manny kept on screaming that his soul had been invaded.

His screams stopped when the guard, emboldened by his dispatching of the other prisoner, knocked him out with a blow to the head. The silence that followed only lasted a second before the guard began to scream. He shrieked for just under a minute before he stopped. His scream was followed by the sound of his body hitting the floor.

Luckily this time none of them were dead. Ironically it was the guard, who had not actually suffered any kind of brutal head trauma, who took the longest to wake up. When he did, he corroborated the two prisoners' version of events. He insisted that he had seen something that to his eyes looked like a dark, sentient cloud—which he insisted had to be a ghost of some kind—leave Manny's body before it flew away through the concrete wall.

Victoria wasn't in a position to hear this directly from the guard's mouth, but the news of the ghost spread quickly enough that she knew of its existence within the hour. If ever there was a moment when she felt most compelled to forget her pride and speak aloud so that she might go free, that was it. The thought that she might face the anger of a spirit of obvious evil was almost enough to make her forget how horrible words sounded when they left her mouth—almost, but not quite. She remained silent, praying quietly in her mind that she would not come face to face with the spirit so terrifying that it had thus far killed one prisoner and sent two others and a guard to the hospital.

*   *   *

Victoria did not sleep that night or the next. Only utter exhaustion allowed her any rest by the third. That was true not just for her, but also for every other prisoner in the jailhouse. The guards were more rested only because they had the luxury of sleeping at their homes, but beyond that, their level of anxiety was the same. Worse than the fear of the dark spirit was the anticipation of its arrival. No one had any idea when it would next appear, and the wait proved torturous. By the fifth day, some people began to hope that the spirit would not appear again. This hope was shattered by a cry in the dark.

Victoria was spared this time, as she was the next, which occurred three days later. She began to believe that her prayers had not been in vain—some grace from above was keeping the spirit from visiting her cell at night—but then, a full week later, she discovered the folly of her faith.

She no longer dreamed of the handsome cavalry officer. Now she simply dreamed of the horse, which she rode across vast distances in her mind. She traveled the entire country in these dreams, delighting in the freedom of her movement and her ability to converse normally with everyone she met. Although she seldom remembered these unconscious fantasies after she woke up, she could still recall the sense of peace and hope that they instilled in her.

But that night the dream was different. As she rode across a great, beautiful plain, the sky above turned dark with heavy black clouds and her horse began to whinny and snort with fear. Thunder began to roll and lightning streaked across the sky as a heavy rain began to fall. Her horse grew uncontrollable and threw her to the sodden ground below. As she lay there, wounded, she looked up and saw the dark clouds swirl and move in a way that made them seem alive. They gathered together into a small, concentrated mass and started moving directly toward her.

Sensing that this was not a dream, Victoria awoke saw the black spirit that had been plaguing the jailhouse floating above her cot. "IT'S IN HERE!" she heard herself scream, too frightened to remain silent or be embarrassed by the pitch of her words. "THE SPIRIT IS IN HERE! GET ME OUT! GET ME OUT BEFORE IT—"

Before she could say another word the dark spirit plunged toward her and disappeared inside her body. She could feel it as it penetrated, and though she had never previously been aware of the exact location of her soul, she could now tell that that was precisely where the spirit was headed.

"GET IT OUT!" she screamed. "GET IT OUT!"

She could hear the sound of running and of keys clanging together as the guard on duty raced to her cell, but rather than relief all she felt was a torment she lacked the vocabulary to describe. It was a pain that did not hurt; a torment that left no wound. The spirit was in her soul; it possessed her completely. And it used that power to tell her something, something that made her scream.

Of all the screams the prisoners had heard in the past few weeks, this was the one they would remember until their dying day. It shattered glass and caused dogs to bark for miles around. It made grown men weep and it almost caused the guard at her cell door to faint. Somehow he managed to stay conscious and gain entry into Victoria's cell. Her screaming would not end, and though it was against everything in his nature to strike a woman, he considered the blow he delivered to her head to be an act of mercy. It silenced her, and the poor guard was forced to watch as the spirit left her quivering body, but this time it did not float away as it had done the other times before. This time it exploded as if the sound of Victoria's scream had made it no longer want to exist.

This time the guard lost his fight to stay vertical and collapsed to the floor in a heap.

When Victoria awoke, she could not speak even if she had wanted to. Her screaming had done so much damage to her vocal chords that they did not let her utter a single whisper for several days. When she could finally speak, she was shocked to hear that the words that came out of her mouth now possessed a sultry, smoky quality that perfectly suited her physical appearance. She kept waiting for this quality to go away, but it soon became clear that the change was permanent. She would have her new voice for the rest of her life.

Overjoyed, she began talking at a rate that would have exhausted even her late husband Charlie. She told everyone she could her explanation for how Charlie died, and when she was finally tried for his murder, she had become an expert in detailing the story to its maximum effect. The all-male jury found her a very sympathetic witness and took only 20 minutes to declare her not guilty of any crime.

She was now a free woman in possession of the small fortune Charlie had made in smart investments over the years. Her money, along with her many other charms, which now included an extremely attractive speaking voice, made Victoria extremely desirable to Madison's handsomest bachelors. She chose to ignore their attentions, however, and used her money to buy a horse and learn how to ride. Once she became proficient, she started to travel—first around the state and then around the country.

During her travels she met a lot of people. All were impressed by her beauty and character, but they also sensed a quality of sadness she refused to explain. None of them knew of what had happened to Victoria that terrifying night at the Madison Jailhouse. They did not know to ask her what it was the spirit had told her when it had taken possession of her, but even if they did know enough to ask, it wouldn't have mattered—the normally talkative woman would have gone immediately silent and not said a word.

It was the only subject on which Victoria now had no comment.

Haunted Mary

Daniel's life was full of stress. His boss was a maniac who made his employees miserable by constantly ignoring what they had to say and insisting on following his own blurred vision, only to blame them when these schemes went awry and the company lost money. His wife was threatening to divorce him because she felt unfulfilled, and his 13-year-old daughter told him at the dinner table the night before that she wanted to be on birth control.

He had never been someone who reacted well to pressure, and there were moments now and then when he considered just running away from his life or even doing something a lot more drastic.

It was lunchtime on a swelteringly hot day in early August. His boss had just chewed him out for getting an important project in on time. "Anyone can meet a deadline," he had been told. "I expect my employees to be passionate enough about their work that they get their projects done days, even weeks, before they have to. It's about drive, Daniel, something you're sorely lacking."

Perhaps his boss was right. Maybe he did lack drive. Maybe that was why his life was so miserable. He considered all of these things as he ate his lunch in front of the Milwaukee River, which he liked to stare at when his mind was distracted by painful or unpleasant thoughts.

Maybe I should just jump in, he thought. *Take a leap into that water and never come back up. No one will miss me, and at least I'll go out knowing that Dottie isn't going to get a penny of life insurance out of it. Let's see how fulfilled she is when she has to work as a waitress to support her sexually promiscuous teenaged daughter.*

Looking out at the river, Daniel put down his sandwich and stood up from the bench he had been sitting on. He walked to the bank of the water and wondered if the warm weather meant that the water was warm as well. *It would be so easy,* he thought. *Just one little step and I'm in.*

This was his "to be or not to be" moment, and he would have given it more time if he hadn't been so suddenly interrupted.

SPPPLLLLLAAAAAAASSSSSSSSSHHHHHHHHHH!!!!

Daniel awoke from the daze of self-absorption and saw that someone nearby had faced the same decision he had been puzzling over and had apparently chosen the "not to be" option. There was a girl, not much older than his own daughter, drowning in the water.

It did not occur to him to even think about what he did next. He jumped into the water and swam to the girl and held her up out of the surprisingly cold water. Just seconds before he had been considering doing exactly what she had done, but now he knew in his heart that life was far too precious to just throw it away.

A crowd gathered as he helped the girl out of the water. The police came with an ambulance and took her away. Everyone congratulated Daniel and called him a hero. He felt so good about what he had done that he went back to work and told his boss that he quit, but not before telling the man what all of his employees thought of him. He then went back home and told his wife that she was free to ful-fill herself and get a job so she could support the family for a change. He told his daughter that if she even thought about having sex, he would send her to an all-girls Catholic school before she had a chance to blink.

As he went to bed that night he realized that he had not been the only person to save a life that day. By showing him the true worth of life and what it meant to him, the girl he had saved had saved him in return. And he didn't even know her name.

It was Mary.

*   *   *

The Spiegel family consisted of only two people, Mary and her father. Mary was 14 and her father was usually too drunk to remember his own name, much less his age. They lived in a tiny hole of an apartment that was filled with cockroaches and mice. It was paid for thanks to her father's disability check, but that was as far as the money went. If they wanted to eat—and they did—then Mary had to work.

She had started working for the widow Golding at the beginning of the summer. She had been going to school before then, but she would not be going back—it was far too hard to keep up her homework and earn enough money to support two people at the same time.

Mrs. Golding ran a boardinghouse that catered to single girls in the big city who couldn't afford to live on their own. She was not a nice woman, and she had a reputation for evicting girls onto the street if they were even a day late in their weekly rent. She had hired Mary to work around the house, doing the jobs that she now found too difficult or unpleasant to undertake in her declining years. The old widow was fully aware of Mary's situation and wasn't above exploiting it when it suited her. Soon after she hired the girl, it wasn't uncommon for her to spend the entire day sitting in her chair in the front living room, reading a cheap paperback while the Mary broke her back trying to keep the house in order.

Sometimes Mrs. Golding did get out of the living room chair, but only so she could sit in one in another part of the house. That afternoon, August 8, 1974, she was in the kitchen baking apple pies. That is to say, she was sitting on a kitchen chair watching Mary bake the pies. She had the girl working on the mixing the pastry when a strange uneasiness came upon the room.

"What did you do?" asked Mrs. Golding.

"Ma'am?" asked Mary.

"Something's wrong in here," the old woman insisted. "I can feel it. I know it's nothing I did, so it must be you."

"It feels normal to me, ma'am."

"Don't be so insolent! If I say something feels odd in here, then something feels odd and you best remember that. I can find another piece of white trash to clean my toilets if I have to, so you show me the proper respect if you know what's good for you."

"Yes, ma'am," Mary said quietly.

"It smells in here," Mrs. Golding went on. "Like rotting eggs. Did you clean the refrigerator like I told you to?"

"Yes, ma'am. I did it yesterday."

"Well you must have done a typically lousy job. I really don't know why I keep you here. For the amount of money I'm paying you, I could get someone who actually wanted to work."

"I want to work, Mrs. Golding."

"A person wouldn't know that by the way you act. And I definitely smell rotting eggs. I've always hated that nasty odor of sulfur. Makes me sick to my stomach."

"I don't smell it, Mrs. Golding."

"Of course you don't. You live in filth so you're used to the scent of it. Decent people who live in clean homes are much more sensitive to the smells of decay."

Mary went to the refrigerator and opened it. "We don't have any eggs in here, ma'am. I used the last one for the pie dough and it was still fresh."

"Don't be so smart," said Mrs. Golding. "Just because I said I smelled rotting eggs, that doesn't mean that rotting eggs are causing what I'm smelling. It could be something else entirely that has the same odor as rotting eggs."

"I'm sorry, ma'am," Mary apologized. "I guess I wasn't thinking."

Mrs. Golding seemed satisfied with Mary's apology and continued her hard work of sitting in the kitchen chair and sipping from a glass of ice-cold lemonade.

Mary returned to beating the dough and started stretching and rolling it out. She found this to be a very enjoyable job, because it allowed her to imagine that the dough was Mrs. Golding's face.

"What are you smiling about, girl?" asked her employer.

"Nothing, ma'am."

"Don't tell me 'nothing.' You don't think I know what you're smiling about? I'm not as stupid as you think I am. Maybe it was stupid of me to hire on someone as ungrateful and ignorant as you, but beyond that my record is clear. Now stop your smiling and get those pies made."

Mary couldn't afford to lose her patience with the old woman, but the constant stream of abuse was definitely taking its toll on her. She stopped smiling, but she did not stop imagining that the dough in her hands represented Mrs. Golding's face. The harder she worked it, the angrier she began to feel. What had she done to deserve to have this be her life? Why couldn't she have been like the other kids she had gone to school with? She couldn't imagine that any of their lives were like this. The more she thought about it, the more unfair it all seemed, and the more unfair it seemed, the harder she pounded the dough.

SLAM!!!!

Both Mary's and Mrs. Golding's heads popped up as the cellar's trapdoor exploded open so violently that it nearly tore itself off of its hinges. Before they could say anything about how strange this was, far stranger things began to happen around them. Silverware soaking in the kitchen sink lifted out of the water and shot dangerously around the room. Dishes started slamming against the walls, and every chair except for the one Mrs. Golding was sitting on started levitating toward the ceiling. Both Mary and Mrs. Golding screamed as they ducked to get out of the way of the flying projectiles.

Their cries and the sound of the breaking dishes were heard by all of the boardinghouse's young female tenants. They left their rooms to investigate what was going on and saw it all happening with their own eyes. It lasted for just over two minutes before, just as suddenly it had started, it ended, and all of the objects that had been floating in the air crashed back down to the ground.

No one knew who called the local news stations, but someone did and they sure came fast. Before they even had time to think about what had happened to them, Mary and Mrs. Golding had microphones and cameras thrust in front of their faces. Both were still so shocked by what they had experienced that neither managed to say anything worth recording on film. The newsmen grumbled about having wasted their time, but the two women were too dazed to care or be offended.

Mrs. Golding was so taken aback by what had happened that she actually allowed Mary to go home early without docking her pay. Mary was so confused by what she had seen that she didn't even consider the consequences of coming home before she was expected.

"What are you doing here?" her father shouted, his breath and body reeking of the cheap red wine her meager earnings paid for.

"Mrs. Golding told me I could leave early," she answered him.

He slapped her hard across her face. "Don't you lie to me," he said to her. "You got fired didn't you? You useless bitch! How hard is it to keep a job?"

"Good question," she mumbled under her breath before she thought better of it.

"What did you say?" he shouted at her.

"Nothing. I didn't say anything," she said. "I didn't get fired, I swear. Something strange happened at the boardinghouse and Mrs. Golding sent me home. That's all that happened, honest."

"It better be," he threatened with a finger poke to her chest. "If you can't contribute, then I don't need you here. Think about that the next time you want to be a wise ass. See how fun it'll be for you to live out on the street."

As bad as living on the street sounded, it was hard for Mary to believe that it could be any worse than where she was.

The next day Mrs. Golding set Mary to work cleaning up the mess made by whatever it was that happened in the kitchen. "And hurry up about it," said the old woman, who seemed to have put the trauma behind her, "you still owe me a pie from yesterday."

"Yes, ma'am," Mary sighed as she started picking up the sharp remnants of the shattered plates. She tried her best not to cut herself on the sharp edges, but she became distracted for a moment and felt a sharp jab of pain as one jagged piece sliced into her right index finger. "Dammit!" she swore as the wound immediately started to bleed. She rushed over to the sink to run it under the tap.

"What are you doing?" asked Mrs. Golding when she saw Mary at the sink.

"I cut myself, ma'am," Mary told her.

"You are just the most useless person ever, aren't you?"

"Those pieces are sharp, Mrs. Golding," Mary defended herself. "Anyone could cut themselves on them."

"You're just full of sass today. Well, let's see how sassy you are when I don't pay you for the time that you missed yesterday."

Mary couldn't believe this. She turned away from the tap and looked her employer in the face. "You told me to go home!" she reminded her.

"I wasn't in my right mind," Mrs. Golding insisted. "But now that I have time to think about it, I don't see why I should have to pay you for time you didn't work."

"But that's not fair!"

"It's fair to me," said the old woman.

Mary's face turned red and the blood from her wound started to spurt out quickly as her heartbeat accelerated from the rage she was feeling.

As if the room could sense her emotions, it started to shake and vibrate. The pieces of broken plates she had failed to pick up lifted off of the floor and started hurtling through the air at extremely dangerous velocities. A large knife that had been left on the counter immediately joined them.

"It's you!" Mrs. Golding shouted at Mary. "You're the one who is doing this."

"No, I'm not!" Mary insisted.

"Get out of here!" the old woman shouted at her. "Get out of here and don't ever come back! You're fired!"

"But—"

"I said you're fired!"

Everything fell to the floor.

Her father beat her when she told him. The only thing that kept him from killing her was that he had become weakened by the effects of his alcoholism. She managed to defend herself and escape out of the apartment before he could inflict any more violence on her.

"And don't you come back!" he shouted at her as she left.

Scared, hurt and confused by the strange events in her already messed-up life, Mary didn't know what to do next. She had no friends she could go to. She had no money. She had nothing but the clothes she was wearing.

Her entire life had been filled with hopelessness, so there was no reason why this moment should feel any different, but it did. For the first time in her short life, it appeared to Mary that things were not going to get better. She had hit rock bottom and that was where she was going to stay.

She had no idea where she was walking or what time it was. The sun was shining and it was hot, but she took no notice of her surroundings. She had no place to go, which freed her to go anyplace she wanted. Had she thought about it, this freedom would have felt like a terrible burden.

She found herself staring at water. It was the Milwaukee River. She wondered if it would be warm on a stiflingly hot day like this. She decided to find out.

It was cold.

She made no attempt to save herself. She did not struggle against the water and allowed it to pull her down. She felt only relief as she began to sink.

But then she felt someone's hands grab her body. They pulled her up and lifted her head out of the water. She saw a middle-aged man, slightly younger than her father. He was dressed in a business suit, which was becoming heavy as it soaked in the water.

She saw people gathering at the bank of the river, watching as the man saved her life. They helped him pull her out of the water and onto the dry ground. She sputtered and gasped as inhaled water escaped from her lungs in favor of breathable air. A policeman arrived and performed CPR. He was followed by an ambulance, which took her away.

It all happened so fast that she was already inside the hospital before she was able to figure out what was going on. Because of her age and their inability to contact her father (he didn't have a telephone), a social worker was called in. He sat by her bed and listened as Mary told him what had happened to her that day.

After hearing her talk about the flying objects in the boardinghouse kitchen, he decided it would be a good idea if she underwent a psychiatric evaluation at the local mental health facility.

*   *   *

Dr. Davis did not think Mary was crazy. She was certainly neurotic and prone to bouts of prolonged sleepwalking, but she was not mentally ill, which made her certainty about what she had seen happen at the boardinghouse all the more interesting. Taking an unusual interest in the case, he decided to interview the women Mary claimed also saw the strange phenomenon.

Mrs. Golding and all of her boarders confirmed Mary's story, and though he was a skeptic about all matters that seemed tinged with the supernatural, something about this case in particular fascinated him.

Knowing little about the world of the paranormal, he contacted local experts to help him come up with different theories about what may have occurred on those two occasions. His personal theory was that nothing supernatural had occurred at all. What happened instead was that everyone was so shocked to see sweet, quiet Mary pushed to the point of a psychotic fit that they interpreted her violent outburst—which included her throwing everything she could get her hands on—as a paranormal phenomenon. He was the first person to admit that this sounded far-fetched, but it was far more plausible than the alternative theories proposed by the paranormal experts.

One bearded gentleman who had written several books about ghosts suggested that what had happened at the boardinghouse was the result of a poltergeist—an angry, uncontrollable spirit that manifests itself in only the most destructive of ways. When the doctor asked the man why, if it was a poltergeist, it had only appeared those two specific times, the expert suggested that sometimes spirits form connections with living people.

"Perhaps what we're dealing with here is not a poltergeist," the man theorized, "but instead a regular spirit that formed a bond with the young girl. Most of the time the spirit does nothing to indicate to the living that it exists, but when it became agitated by the harsh treatment of the girl it had bonded with, it showed itself in the most extreme manner possible."

Another expert, this time an older woman who had made it her life's work to study psychic phenomena, suggested that Mary was a telepath—a person with the ability to move objects with her mind—whose latent abilities only came out during moments of emotional distress.

"She's still very young, so it is likely that she is only capable of exhibiting these abilities randomly and without being aware that she is responsible for what is happening when they affect the world around her. My guess is that her powers remained latent throughout her childhood, and it is only her recent ascent into womanhood that has allowed them to finally show themselves."

Dr. Davis found both of these theories intriguing. They were also highly implausible and without any scientific basis whatsoever. If the first theory was true, then he wondered why the suggested spirit chose to bond with Mary and not someone else. Also, he wondered why it only reacted the way it did on those two occasions, when she faced similar and often worse treatment at the boarding-house nearly every day. And if the second theory was true, then why had Mary's telepathic abilities not shown them-selves in the other stressful moments of her life? Surely they would have appeared at some point during one of the many times she was beaten by her father.

Without having come any closer to anything approach-ing a satisfactory answer, Dr. Davis decided to take his investigation to the next level. He would have to test the two different theories for himself.

*   *   *

Mary had grown used to her regular sessions with the doctor. In the beginning she had been shy and hesitant to talk to him, but as time went on he earned her trust and she opened up to him. Today Dr. Davis knew he risked los-ing that trust, perhaps forever, but—after some long con-sideration—he decided that was a risk he was willing to take.

The session started like any other. Mary came in and sat down at the chair in front of his desk. The time at the hospital was doing her good physically. Her skinny, mal-nourished frame was filling out, and the face of a pretty girl was beginning to show itself from behind her long black bangs.

"Hi, Mary," he greeted her, "how are you feeling today?"

"I'm good, Dr. Davis," she answered him honestly. "According to the night nurse I didn't get up from my bed once last night."

"I know," he smiled, "she told me. We've discussed how it might be possible that you started sleepwalking as a way to get away from your nightmares. Did you have one last night?"

"No," she answered with a smile. "I had a good dream."

"Really? What was it about?"

"I was back in school—but a different one where no one knew who I was, and even though it was my first day I was making friends with the other students."

"That does sound like a good dream. Do you want to go back to school?"

"Yes. I don't like being stupid."

Dr. Davis shook his head at this. "I've told you before," he chided her, "you are not stupid. A lack of education is completely different than a lack of intelligence. You're a very smart girl, you just haven't had any opportunities to take advantage of what you're capable of."

"I suppose," she said haltingly. She wasn't convinced he was right.

The doctor found himself having to take a deep breath. He wasn't sure if he could go on with what he had planned for this session. Perhaps not knowing the whole truth of her case was preferable to the potential damage finding it out could conceivably have on the girl.

Mary sensed his hesitancy. "Is something wrong, Dr. Davis?" she asked him.

He looked at her and decided in that moment that she was too strong to break as easily as he feared—her scar tissue was too thick. She may never trust him again, but she would survive and continue on without him.

"Mary," he said to her, "I want to do something with you called role-playing. Do you know what that is?"

"It's like we pretend to be other people, right?"

"Yes and no. I want you to be you, but I'm going to act like several people you know. What I want you to do is act the way you did when you were with these people. Don't react to them the way you would now, but instead try and remember how you would react to them back then, before you came to the hospital. Can you do that?"

"I think so."

"First I'm going to pretend to be your father. Is that all right?"

"I guess."

Dr. Davis took a second before he took on the harsh tone of her alcoholic father. "What good are you to me if you can't bring in any cash?" he slurred at her.

Mary stayed quiet.

"You don't think I keep you around for your conversation, do you? Because I've had better talks with empty pizza boxes, I tell you that! I swear to you, girlie, if you don't find a way to pay for your keep, then I'll just get rid of you without it worrying me for a second. I got rid of your no-good mother, so there's nothing stopping me from doing the same to you!"

Mary didn't say a word.

"Say something, dammit!" he swore at her, but she remained mute.

"That was very good," he said, changing his tone back to his regular voice. "How did you feel when that was happening."

"Angry," she admitted right away.

"But you didn't say anything."

"No, because I knew it wouldn't make things better if I did. You would just get meaner and start hitting me—I mean," she corrected herself, "*my dad* would get meaner and start hitting me."

Mary was reacting much better to this treatment than he had thought—perhaps she was making real progress after all. That was good news, even if it meant certain questions would remain unanswered.

"Okay, now I'm going to pretend to be your boss, Mrs. Golding. Do you think you can handle that?"

"I think so."

Once again, Dr. Davis paused as he got into character. "I really don't know why I was dumb enough to hire you," he said in a voice that approximated an old woman's. "You're slow, you don't listen and instead of saving time by having you around I have to spend every second watching you to make sure you do what you're supposed to. Isn't that right?"

"Yes, ma'am. If you say so."

"I do say so. You really are more trouble than you're worth. The only reason I keep you around is because you're so cheap and I feel sorry for you. You're lucky I'm such a charitable person—you should show me a lot more gratitude. If you had been raised right you'd know enough to thank me for what I do for you."

Dr. Davis could see that he was pushing Mary's buttons. She had managed to stay calm during the insults that were supposedly from her father, but there was something about the way Mrs. Golding spoke to her that caused her anger to rise much closer to her surface.

"Well," he pushed her, "aren't you going to thank me?"

He could see that Mary wanted to throttle him, but she didn't. Instead she swallowed her emotions and only said, "Thank you, ma'am," in a quiet, unhappy voice.

"That's enough role-playing for today," he decided, switching back to his normal voice. "I could see that you were getting very angry there at the end. Why didn't I see the same thing when I pretended to be your father?"

"Because," she thought about it, "he acted that way because he was sick and sad. All he had in his life was his drinking, so when he hurt me it was just another way for him to hurt himself, but with Mrs. Golding it's different. She just acts that way because she's a cruel, mean person who enjoys seeing another person suffer. She is," Mary's cheeks blushed over the word she was about to say, "a *bitch*."

That was all the time they had for today's session. Mary got up and started walking out of her doctor's office. She was at the door when she stopped and spoke to him. "Dr. Davis," she said, "I don't think I like role-playing very much."

"Don't worry," he answered back. "We won't do it again."

So what had he learned from this?

He had learned that Mary's emotional reaction to abuse depended on her feelings for her abuser. She did not react strongly to her father's attacks because she thought he was pathetic and pitiable, but she found it difficult to stay quiet when faced by the taunts of a sadist such as Mrs. Golding. He had hoped that sometime during their role-playing she would have gotten angry enough at him for something similar to what had happened at the boardinghouse to occur. Either he couldn't make her that emotional, or he was right all along and the incident as it was described by those who saw it was nothing more than an attempt to explain the shocking outburst of a shy, quiet young girl.

His little experiment failed to give him any of the answers he wanted. It seemed clear that there was only one thing left for him to do.

He would take her back to the boardinghouse.

*   *   *

Mary was at first reluctant to return to the house of her former employer. Not because she was afraid of suffering through another paranormal attack, but because she didn't want to see Mrs. Golding ever again. In the end she agreed to go when her doctor convinced her that it would help her treatment and assured her that she was free to speak to Mrs. Golding anyway she liked.

Mary wasn't the only person who wasn't thrilled with the idea of this visit. Nothing out of the normal had happened at the boardinghouse since Mrs. Golding had fired Mary all those months ago, and she wanted to keep it that way. It took a signed check for $250 and a promise to pay for any damage the house suffered while Mary was there before she agreed to allow them to come over.

"You're getting fat," were the first words the old woman spoke to the girl when they arrived. "They must be feeding you too much at that booby hatch they're keeping you at."

Mary looked over at her doctor. He gave her an approving nod.

"You can say all you want to me, Mrs. Golding," she said politely, "but that doesn't mean I have to listen. All you do when you say those things is prove to everyone what an awful person you really are."

"Why—" Mrs. Golding started, shocked that the young girl had spoken to her like that, but before she could complete her statement, Mary and the doctor left her alone and walked to the kitchen.

"So this is where it happened?" he asked her.

"Yes," she answered him with a nod.

"What were you feeling when it happened?"

"I was angry. Really angry," she told him.

"Why?"

"Because no matter how hard I tried to be good, all I got was people telling me how rotten I was."

"What did you do with your anger?"

"I just kept it inside me. I knew it wouldn't do me any good if I let it all out."

"But you did let it out."

"What do you mean?"

"Think about it, Mary," he told her. "The only two times the incidents here happened were during moments when you felt incredible anger and hatred for a person who kept you around only so she could have someone to belittle and order around. Has it never occurred to you that you were the one responsible for what everyone saw?"

"No," she answered him honestly, "it never has."

"And why is that?"

"Because I wasn't."

"How can you be so sure?"

"Because I know who did it," she answered him with hesitation.

"What?"

"I've always known. I knew before it happened."

"Mary, what are you saying?" asked her doctor. "Who else could be responsible for what happened here?"

"Mr. Golding, of course," she answered him.

*   *   *

Mary had been working there for a week when she heard the whispering in her ear. *Get away from her*, it had urged, *before it's too late.*

"Too late for what?" she asked aloud, but she was alone and there was no one around to answer her.

The next time she heard it was the first time Mrs. Golding berated her for what she felt was insufficient dusting of the draperies. *It won't get any better*, the voice told her. *She'll keep on you like this until she breaks you. That's what she does. That's what she did to me.*

As time went on the whisper in her ear told her more and more about the woman she worked for. For a long time she didn't know who was doing the telling, but then one day she was cleaning in Mrs. Golding's closet and found an old book of photographs. They were all black and white and—based on the clothes the people in them were wearing—had been taken in the 1940s. Mary was shocked when she realized that the young, pretty woman who was in most of the pictures was her employer—she had never considered that there might have once been a time when the old woman was attractive.

In almost just as many pictures she saw a small, balding man with a bushy mustache and a shy, endearing smile. *That's me*, the whisper told her, *back when I was happy. It didn't last long.* This statement seemed to be proven by the photographs in the book. In the beginning they depicted a young and happy couple, but as they went on the genuine smiles faded away and were replaced by the kind of polite grins unhappy people use when a camera is pointed at them. By the end of the book, no one was even pretending to smile. *Nothing I did was good enough for her*, the whisperer complained to Mary. *She criticized and belittled everything I did. I couldn't take it anymore. I threw myself into the river to escape her. Make my words, if you stay here long enough, you will too.*

*　　*　　*

"And he was right," Mary told her doctor. "I did."

"Mary…" Dr. Davis tried to think of something to say but was at a loss for words. What she was describing sounded like a classic symptom of schizophrenia, but nothing in his past treatment of her suggested that she suffered from that particular condition.

"I've always known that it was Mr. Golding who caused the dishes and silverware and chairs to fly around the room. The way Mrs. Golding spoke to me reminded his spirit of the way she treated him. It got to a point where he simply couldn't take it any more, so he did something about it. At the time I was mad at him because what he did got me fired, but now I know he was acting in my best interest and did the right thing. Because I got fired, my dad threw me out and that led me to trying to kill myself by jumping into the river, but I was saved by that nice stranger, whoever he was, and I got sent to you and I've never been happier in all of my life. There was a time when I didn't even know I had nightmares because those bad dreams weren't any worse than my everyday life, but now all I have are good dreams about a future I might actually have someday. I can see now that I have the ghost who kept whispering in my ear to thank for that. Mr. Golding saved me."

"That bum saved you?" Mrs. Golding's voiced screeched unpleasantly behind them. "He died 15 years before you were even born—all he saved were the little fishies that chewed him up before his body floated up to the surface of the river. He was a bum. He couldn't do anything right, and I can't tell you how happy I was the day I saw him buried."

"You shouldn't talk about him like that, Mrs. Golding," Mary said quietly.

"Don't you tell me how to talk when you're a guest in my house!" Mrs. Golding snapped at her. "That's the thing about trash like you, you don't know anything about manners. It's a shame that father of yours didn't beat some politeness into you before he drank himself to death."

"Shut up, you old witch!" Mary shouted at her.

"That's it!" roared Mrs. Golding. "Get out of my house! I don't care how much you paid me, it's not worth having this ungrateful waste of space disturbing the sanctity of my home!"

"You really shouldn't talk like that," Mary repeated, "you just get him angrier and angrier when you do."

"Listen to her. She's nuts! I don't want a crazy person in my house! Get out or I'll call the cops. Just you see if I don't!"

Her shrill words were still echoing through the kitchen when a plate shot off the counter and slammed against the wall, where it shattered into dozens of very sharp pieces of shrapnel.

"Dr. Davis, get down!" Mary shouted at the doctor as the first plate was soon followed by others, along with pieces of silverware, loose appliances and some of the room's furniture.

Just as before, the noise aroused the attention of the house's boarders, who arrived in time to witness a melee that made the previous two look like tea parties. The attack was so ferocious that Dr. Davis had to close his eyes for fear of being blinded by one of the objects flying through the air.

It lasted for five whole minutes before the spirit responsible for the mayhem appeared to run out of steam— everything that had been in the air dropped down to the ground with an ear-splitting crash.

"Mrs. Golding?" asked one of the boarders when she saw the old woman lying quietly on the kitchen floor. "Are you okay?"

The old woman did not answer her.

Dr. Davis got up and ran to her. She had no pulse

"Call an ambulance!" he shouted to no one in particular.

The paramedics came, but there was nothing they could do. The heart attack that had hit her during the ghostly attack on her kitchen was so powerful that it killed her on the spot.

No one mourned her passing.

*   *   *

Mary went into foster care following her release from the hospital. For some kids with her history this sometimes meant being sent into another form of hell, but she—for once—was lucky. The family she was sent to was kind and loving, and they adored Mary. Within six months they had decided to adopt her into their family.

She did well at school and did her best to put her first 14 years behind her. Dr. Davis kept in touch with her and was delighted to watch as she grew into an exceptionally bright and talented young woman.

At last all of her nightmares were over and she never heard a voice whisper into her ear ever again.

The Christmas Quilt

It was a cold December night in the town of Poy Sippi, the kind of cold that creeps into every building no matter how high up the thermostat is turned. Florence Delfosse had hers turned up as high as it would go, but she still found herself shivering underneath her blankets as she tried to get to sleep that night. After an hour, she decided that something had to be done if she was going to get any rest before the morning, so she mentally listed some options.

She could put on more clothes, but she always hated the way they bunched up and tangled as she moved around during the night. She could fish out her old electric blanket, but the last time she used it she was fairly certain she smelled smoke, and being warm was one thing, but being burned alive was another. She then remembered the box in her hallway closet. She hadn't touched it or thought about it in years, but she knew that inside of it was an old quilt that was considered something of a mystery by her family.

Florence's mother had found it in 1972, the year they moved into the house. She had found it in the same closet it currently resided in and had assumed it belonged to the former owners, but when she tried to return it to them they insisted that they had never seen it before, and it wasn't theirs to take. She asked them how it had ended up stuck in their closet, and they insisted that they had no idea, which everyone she told the story to agreed was more than a little strange. The quilt was very large and extremely colorful, so much so that you would literally have to be blind not to notice it if it was in front of you.

Curious, Mrs. Delfosse actually took the trouble to have it appraised by an antique dealer, who told her that it was worth thousands of dollars, which was why she had stuck it in a box and put it back into the closet where she had found it. The idea of actually sleeping under something that expensive made her uncomfortable.

But Florence was not her mother, and she had no problem whatsoever sleeping under such an expensive piece of bedding, especially if it kept the chills from creeping into her tired bones. With a yawn, she got out of bed, went to the closet and took out the box that contained the quilt.

This thing is heavy, she thought, when the weight of it took her by surprise. She carried the box to her room, dropped it on the floor and opened it. She lifted out the folded quilt, placed it on the bed and started unfolding it. It was even bigger than she remembered and could have easily covered a bed three or four times larger than her own. She flattened it out with her hand, getting rid of any bumps or folds that might annoy her as she tried to sleep, and then crawled underneath it.

"That's more like it," she sighed as the warmth of the heavy blanket was immediately apparent. No longer cold, she drifted comfortably to sleep in a matter of minutes.

But three hours later, a sudden, inexplicable shout in the darkness of her room wrested her from her slumber. "Give me back my Christmas quilt!" a loud, unidentifiable voice angrily ordered her.

"What the—" Florence said sleepily, uncertain if she had really heard something or had merely dreamed it. "Who said that?"

"Give me back my Christmas quilt!" the voice repeated.

She sat up in her bed and saw that she appeared to be alone in the room, but the sound of the other person's voice suggested otherwise. Most people would find themselves extremely frightened and unnerved by the presence of a disembodied voice in their bedroom, but Florence was too tired and annoyed to react in so typical a manner. Plus, it helped that she was fairly certain she was still asleep and just dreaming all of this.

"Give me back my Christmas quilt!" the voice once again demanded.

"No," she answered back. "I'm using it." With that said, she lay back down and closed her eyes, assuming the matter was settled.

But apparently it wasn't, because at that moment she felt the quilt start to slide right off of her body.

"Stop that!" she protested angrily as she grabbed the quilt and pulled it back up to her chin.

"Give me back my Christmas quilt!" the voice said once again.

"Go away!" Florence shouted back. "I'm trying to sleep!"

For the next three hours Florence engaged in a constant tug of war with the invisible spirit. During all that time it kept repeating the same demand over and over again: "Give me back my Christmas quilt!"

Finally her alarm clock rang, which must have frightened the spirit away because it immediately let go of the quilt and didn't say another word. It was only then that Florence became frightened, realizing at that moment that she had actually been awake the whole time and that the past three hours had not been a dream.

Lying underneath the warmth of the expensive mystery quilt, she then proceeded to completely freak out.

*   *   *

The Delfosses were a generous, open-minded kind of family, so when Florence told her sister what had happened to her during the previous night, Dinah did not suggest that she go take a trip over to the Funny Farm.

"I bet that's why the original owners of the house told Mom that they hadn't seen the quilt before—they knew it was haunted," suggested Dinah.

"Well, that's just totally rude," said Florence.

"I don't see what the big deal is," said Joey, Dinah's boyfriend. "Just put the thing back in the closet and forget about it. If there is a ghost—and that's a *big* if—it only seems to care about the quilt when someone else is using it."

"I don't care," said Florence, "I don't want that thing in the same house as me."

"Then throw the quilt away," said Dinah.

"I can't do that," Florence protested. "Do you know how much it's worth?"

"Then sell it."

"Okay, but what do I do until then?"

"I'll take it," said Joey.

"Really? You'll do that for me?"

"Sure," he said. "It doesn't seem like that big a deal."

"Don't kid yourself," said Florence. "When you find yourself fighting over a quilt with a ghost in your bedroom for three hours, you'll realize what a big deal it really is."

*   *   *

Joey took the quilt home with him and set it on his kitchen table, where it stayed until around 11:30 PM, when he started feeling a chill that just didn't want to go away as he lay beneath the covers of his bed. It only took a single shiver for him to get out of bed and grab the quilt off of the table. He hesitated for only a second before he threw it down upon his bed, deciding that—at the very least—this would be a good test to see if he was dating someone with a crazy person in her family.

It took only half an hour for him to find out that he wasn't.

His alarm clock had barely reached midnight when he felt the quilt start to slide off of him.

Holy crap! Joey swore to himself, realizing that Florence had been telling the truth all along. He held on to the quilt, expecting the struggle to last a lot longer than it did, but the ghost appeared to give up after only 15 minutes. It also stayed silent, never once ordering him to give the quilt back to it.

After an hour passed without further incident, Joey figured that the whole thing was over with. Then he heard the sound of his doorbell ringing repeatedly, as if someone was pressing down on it and wasn't going to stop until he got up and answered the door.

"What the hell is going on?" he wondered as he got out of bed and slipped on his bathrobe. He stumbled in the darkness of his house to his front door, stubbing his big toe along the way. By the time he reached the door he had managed to become very angry and was ready to tear a strip off of whoever was standing on his doorstop.

"What the hell do—" he started to say as he opened the door, but he fell silent at the sight of the face he saw staring at him from the outside. Or, to be more precise, he was silenced by the *complete lack of a face* that he saw staring back at him. There, dressed in a black suit that was at least 40 years out of style, was a man without a face. There was nothing but a wall of skin where his eyes, nose, mouth and various other facial features were supposed to be.

Joey's response to seeing such a sight was to scream—very loudly.

If the faceless spirit's intention was to retrieve the quilt, it failed, largely because it was frightened away by Joey's extreme reaction to its appearance, but also because it lacked the mouth required to ask for it.

The spirit turned away and vanished; Joey kept screaming for at least another 30 seconds. He then slammed the door shut, ran to his room and ripped the quilt off of his bed and stuffed it into his hallway closet, where it stayed until he took it back to Florence in the morning.

She had to hold onto it for only a few days until she found someone who was willing to buy it at its fair market value. As she handed it over she wrestled with her conscience over whether or not to mention its haunted history. In the end she chose to stay quiet for two reasons.

The first was that she figured the buyer would think she was crazy and never believe her. The second was that she now agreed with her mother that anyone crazy enough to actually put a quilt that expensive on top of a bed deserved to be haunted by it.

4
Just Plain Haunted

Turnabout is Fair Play

When it came to his farm, August Heinz's senses were nearly superhuman. Such was his concern for the land and animals that allowed him to provide for his wife and three children that he had developed a connection with them that bordered on the psychic. That was why, as he lay in his bed one cold February night in 1925, he awoke from the soundest of sleeps when the distant smell of smoke briefly tickled his nose.

"The hay barn!" he cried out, though there was no possible way he could have known the source of the smoky smell. He jumped out of his bed and ran outside in his nightclothes. There he saw that his hay barn was indeed being consumed by a rapidly growing blaze.

"Charlie! Freddy!" he shouted, calling out for his two teenaged sons. "Wake up and get out here! You hear me? Charlie! Freddy!"

Both of his sons heard their father's shouts and, smelling the now stronger odor of smoke in the air, they leapt out of their beds and ran outside.

"The barn's on fire!" shouted Freddy, too caught up in the moment to be embarrassed by the obviousness of his statement.

"I need one of you to grab one of the horses and ride to our neighbors and tell them we'll need help stopping this fire before it spreads," their father told them.

"Yes, sir," said Charlie, who at 19 was the older of the two boys by two years. He then immediately did what he was told and ran off in search of his horse.

"August? What's going on?" August heard his wife, Patricia, speak from the doorway of their small two-story farmhouse. "Why are you shouting?"

"Come outside and see for yourself," he answered.

"Oh my word!" she exclaimed when she saw their burning hay barn. "I'll go wake Elizabeth," she said, referring to their 21-year-old daughter, who was such a sound sleeper they could have been shouting right beside her and not have roused her with their cries.

As she ran back inside their house, August and Freddy ran toward the blazing hot inferno that used to be their hay barn. It was clear that there was nothing the two of them could do alone to stop the fire, but they might be able to slow it down if they kept dousing it with buckets of water from their nearby well.

Fueled by the adrenaline that comes during such situations, the two of them managed to keep this up for almost a full hour before they became so tired they had to stop. During that time Patricia and Elizabeth had joined the fire brigade, but even with four people they were doing little more than keeping the fire at a standstill.

Slowly, their neighbors—having been alerted to the situation by Charlie—began to arrive, and soon, enough had arrived to form a proper bucket chain. It took a lot of hard work, but as the sun started to rise, ushering in the new day, the fire had finally been quelled and had been kept from spreading to the Heinz's home or the second barn where they kept their livestock.

Once the fire had been beaten, the family completed the chores that could not be skipped even for one day, no matter what the reason. Only then were they able to get the rest they had been denied that night—and only then did they have time to think about what may have caused the fire in the first place.

The most likely cause would usually have been a bolt of lightning, but there had been no storm that night or any night for almost that entire winter. They never kept any oil lamps burning in the barn at night, so that too could be dismissed as a cause, which left only the disturbing possibility that the fire was not an accident, but a deliberate case of arson. The problem with this explanation was that the Heinzes were good, kind folk who had never made an enemy in their entire lives, which led them to arrive at the frightening conclusion that this was a random act committed by a madman.

They warned their neighbors in the farming community just outside of Portage, to be on the lookout for such a man; it was likely that he could strike again anywhere at any time. But as the months passed, it began to appear that this incident was an isolated one. Then in the beginning of that June another barn was set ablaze, but instead of proving the existence of a fire-obsessed lunatic in their midst, this second act of arson proved that the Heinzes had, unwittingly, made at least one enemy—it was their second barn that was destroyed.

Although the first fire had been a very unpleasant experience, this second one was devastating. They had been able to save several of their animals from the flames, but many more were killed in the fire, including Charlie's beloved horse. Reeling from this both emotionally and financially devastating loss, the family now had to deal with the very disturbing idea that someone was targeting them for misfortune, and they had no idea who it was. They did not know which was worse—the paranoia that came from not knowing what was going to happen next or the confusion that came from having no idea what they had done to deserve such treatment.

Little did they know that there was something even more terrifying about the situation they were in—a shocking truth they would only gradually be able to accept as their lives continued on.

*   *   *

Before the two fires, suppertime had always been the most important part of the Heinzes' day. As they ate, they would talk about what had happened to them that day, gossip about their neighbors and repeat jokes they had been telling each other for the past 10 years. But this all changed following the destruction of their two barns and the death of most of their livestock. Sadness fell upon the house, and no one had the strength of spirit to gossip or tell jokes anymore.

Instead they sat and ate in a miserable silence that was punctuated only with the sound of clattering cutlery. Three weeks passed without a single word spoken at the table. It took until the end of the month before something happened to rouse them out of their torpor. They were midway through a meal of leftover stew when—from up above their heads—they heard the sound of footsteps.

August's head popped up. He looked around the table and did a quick headcount. Everyone was there and accounted for. "Who could that be?" he asked aloud.

His family answered him with a collective shrug.

As the sound of the footsteps continued, they all looked up at the ceiling above their heads. "Could be a burglar," said Freddie.

"What kind of burglar robs a house when the whole family that lives there is at home?" asked Charlie.

"I don't know," admitted Freddie. "A bad one?"

"August!" Patricia said in a loud, frightened whisper. "What if it's the person responsible for burning down our barns?"

The thought sent a chill down everyone's spine. A burglar—even a really bad one—could be expected to act sensibly when confronted, but the same could not be said for a madman with a seemingly irrational grudge against the family.

"Charlie," August whispered to his eldest son, "fetch me my shotgun."

The family waited silently as Charlie got up to do as he was asked. Up above them the footsteps continued to be heard.

"Here you go," Charlie said to his father as he handed over the large shotgun that had previously been used only to put down farm animals and shoot the occasional deer.

"August, I'm scared," said Patricia.

"It's probably nothing," August lied, "but if someone is up there, I'll scare him away before you can clap your hands twice."

"Do you want us to come with you?" asked Freddie.

"No," August shook his head, "stay here with your mother and sister. I'll be down right away."

That said, the eldest Heinz brandished his shotgun in front of him, his finger on the trigger, and walked up the stairs to the small house's second story. It was dark, too dark to see. Needing some form of light, he hesitantly put down his shotgun and lit an oil lamp. He then tried his best to hold both the lamp and the shotgun in as threatening a manner as he could manage.

Now that he could see, August searched the entire second story for the source of the footsteps, which he could no longer hear. It didn't take him long to conclude that he was the only person up there. Confused, he blew out the lamp and walked back downstairs.

"What happened?" asked Patricia. "We didn't hear a thing!"

"There's no one up there," August told them.

"But what about those footsteps?" asked Elizabeth.

"I can't explain it," said August, "but I can assure you that I was the only person up there."

He put down his shotgun and sat back down at his spot at the table and returned to eating his unfinished meal. Slowly, his extremely spooked family joined him, and they finished their supper without saying another word to each other.

*   *   *

Three months passed, and during that time, the family's quiet meals were invariably interrupted by the same sound of footsteps from up above their heads. For the first week or so, August had grabbed his shotgun and investigated the second story of the house just like he had that first night, but each time he did he ended up with the same result as before. These fruitless searches proved so frustrating that he eventually gave them up and—along with the rest of his family—ignored the sounds from up above.

But not long after their fear had turned into uneasiness, they found themselves confronted with another strange puzzle to challenge their rational minds.

It began one morning when Patricia left the house to start her chores and discovered that the broom she kept in the outside summer kitchen wasn't where she always left it. A creature of habit, it wasn't like her to misplace things, so she assumed that one of the children or her husband must have used it and left it somewhere other than her usual spot. But when she asked them about it, they all denied using it. She went to look for it and eventually found it hidden in an upstairs closet in the main house.

Despite the strange things that were happening around the farm during that time, she was convinced that this had been a prank played on her by one of her children—most likely Freddy, who was the most mischievous of the three. He insisted that he had had nothing to do with the missing broom, as did his brother and sister. But when the broom went missing again the next morning, she refused to accept that there was a potentially more sinister reason for its disappearance.

"Where did you put it, Freddy?" she awoke her son as he lay comfortably underneath his covers.

"Put what?" her son asked sleepily, half convinced he was dreaming the conversation.

"My broom!"

"I didn't put it anywhere," he insisted.

"Don't you lie to me! You're not too old for me to give you a good whack if I have to. I don't have the patience for this, so you tell me where you put it right now!"

By this point Freddy knew he was really talking to his mother, so, with a long yawn, he sat up in his bed and looked her in the eyes with a gaze of unimpeachable sincerity. "Mom, I honestly did not touch your broom, and I'm ashamed that you seem so reluctant to believe me. I'm 17! I'm far too old to pull such childish pranks, especially on someone who I love as much as my mother."

Patricia's resolve instantly turned to mush and she apologized to her son for accusing him of doing something so infantile. Eventually she found the broom hidden underneath some firewood.

For the next three weeks the broom continued to disappear every morning, only to turn up later in a spot that changed every day. Freddy, Charlie and Elizabeth continued to protest their innocence, and given the other strange occurrences at the farm, August and Patricia had little choice but to believe them. Finally, August came up with an idea that, if it didn't solve their problem, would at least give them an idea of what they were dealing with.

He took the broom and—with a long length of sturdy chain—shackled it against a wall in the summer kitchen. He then had Charlie come in and try to take it, but it was secured well enough to the wall that it could not be moved. Satisfied with this part of the plan, August then used a heavy padlock to lock the summer kitchen's only door. Because its windows were too small for a person to climb through, the door was the only way to get inside the kitchen. This could not be done without opening the padlock, and August had the only key.

That next morning he woke up before his wife so he could check to see if his actions had been successful in stopping the phantom broom mover. When he got to the summer kitchen he saw that the padlock on its door had not been touched. With a smile of satisfaction, he opened it and walked inside the kitchen and nearly fainted when he saw that the broom was missing and the chain he had used to secure it to the wall lay broken in pieces on the floor. As he returned to the house to inform his family of what had happened, he found the broom lying on the ground outside the main house's back door.

When he told his wife and children of how the padlock and chain had not been able to deter the mysterious broom thief, they all looked shocked, but Freddy was the only one who reacted strongly enough to the news to faint right where he was standing. It would take a few minutes before he had the strength to fill everyone in on the extremity of his reaction.

"I'm sorry, Mama," he apologized to his mother, "but I just thought it was too funny."

"What are you talking about, Freddy?" his mother asked him.

"When you told me to admit that I was the one who was moving the broom, I insisted that I hadn't touched it, but I was lying. I've been moving the broom all along, until this morning. I figured I'd be found out once it was clear that Dad's trick had kept the broom in its place, but it didn't, which means…" He couldn't complete the sentence.

*　　　*　　　*

The Heinzes now had no doubt that a spirit whose identity was a complete mystery was tormenting them. Footsteps and stolen brooms were one thing, but this phantom among them was the most likely suspect behind the two burned-down barns, which meant that it was clearly angry at them for some reason, and it was only a matter of time before it did something similarly violent again.

Who did they know who had died and who would have cause to return from the grave with a desire for revenge? Did they have living enemies? But the Heinzes came up with no one. They knew little about the history of the land they were on, which meant that if it was a former inhabitant of the farm who was displeased with their presence for some reason, they had no hope of identifying who it was.

But after a while it became clear that their problem wasn't figuring out who the ghost was, but how to get rid of it. The Heinzes were not well versed in the supernatural and knew little of the ways of spirits. Afraid that they would be considered fools, they refused to share their problem with their neighbors, possibly denying themselves some helpful advice.

The family was prepared to suffer "the thing" (as they had taken to calling it) in silence, when finally their salvation came from an unlikely source.

August's brother Klaus was nothing at all like August. While August was a quiet, sober family man who believed in the benefits of a strong work ethic and a good day's labor, Klaus was a drinker and a womanizer who constantly tried to find ways to acquire money without having earned it. Still, despite their differences, the two brothers loved each other and frequently spent time together going out hunting.

One of these hunting trips occurred not long after the broom incident. During the outing, August said nothing to his brother about the strange experiences he and his family had been having over the past few months, but

Klaus could tell he was preoccupied; it was obvious when August missed a clear shot at a deer that he normally would have never failed to capitalize on.

Thanks to that missed shot, the two men returned to August's home empty-handed, but the lack of fresh meat did not keep Patricia from making them a fine meal for their supper. When it was served, Klaus thanked his sister-in-law for her efforts and couldn't help but notice that his relatives were much less gregarious around the table than usual. He was about to comment on this unusual sobriety when he heard the sound of footsteps coming from the ceiling. "Do you hear that?" he asked his relatives.

"Pay it no mind," said August as he continued to eat.

"So you know who is up there, then?" Klaus refused to let the matter go.

"Yes," answered his brother. "No one."

"What do you mean?"

"What he means, Uncle Klaus," Elizabeth told him, "is that as far as we know, no physical being is up there."

"What do you mean by 'physical being'? Are you saying that there's something up there that doesn't have a body?"

"As far as we can tell," admitted Charlie.

"You mean a ghost?"

The entire family shrugged, none of them wanting to say the word aloud.

"What have you done to try to get rid of it?"

"Nothing," said Freddy. "What can we do?"

"Well, how's about giving it a taste of its own medicine?"

"What do you mean?" asked Patricia.

"I bet the blasted thing has been scaring you for ages now. Am I right?"

They all admitted that he was.

"Then what you have to do is scare it right back. Show it that you're not to be trifled with."

"How are we supposed to do that?" asked August.

"I don't know," said Klaus. "Take a shot at it."

"What good would that do?" asked Freddy. "The thing's already dead."

"Yes," said his uncle, "but maybe it doesn't know that."

To prove his point, Klaus got up and grabbed his shotgun.

"Klaus," said August, "you're not going to shoot that gun inside the house, are you?"

"Don't worry, August," Klaus said with a smile, "it isn't loaded." He started walking up the stairs to the second story, then stopped and aimed the gun in the direction of the footsteps. "Hey ghostie!" he shouted at the spirit. "Enjoy this!" Klaus pulled the trigger, and no one was more surprised than he was when a loud blast was heard and a shot fired out of his "unloaded" weapon.

"What did you do?" August shouted worriedly, afraid that his irresponsible brother had just done some considerable damage to his home. But as he rushed from his seat to investigate, he was shocked to find that there was no evidence of the shot having been fired at all. There were no new, unwanted holes anywhere.

"How—" he started to ask, but Freddy interrupted him.

"Do you hear that?" his youngest son asked everyone.

Everyone listened carefully, and soon they all heard what Freddy was referring to. It was a pathetic whimpering sound coming from the fruit cellar.

Charlie opened the cellar door and went down to investigate. There was no one there, and the sound of the whimpering had stopped.

"Told you I could scare it," Klaus said triumphantly.

And scare it he had. After that night the mysterious spirit never troubled the Heinzes ever again. They never did find out where it had come from or why it had focused its attention on them, but from that point on they all knew what they had to do if it ever came back.

Summerwind

"Yeah, fine, whatever," Ginger sighed. "I hope you get better soon," she told the painter on the other end on the phone. "And then I hope you get hit by a bus," she added after she had hung up on him.

"Are you kidding me?" said her husband, Arnold. "Another one?"

"He came down with chicken pox," she answered him. "This is nuts," she declared. "In what universe is it this hard to get someone to come and do some work on your house?"

In the time since the Hinshaws had bought Summerwind, repairman after repairman had cancelled on them for an increasingly varied series of reasons. The man they had hired to do some wallpapering lost three fingers on his right hand in an on-the-job accident that was so bizarre, even he couldn't explain how it happened. A plumber was forced to cancel when he was struck by a case of hysterical blindness caused by the grief he experienced following the death of his beloved shih tzu, Howie. One of the many painters they had tried to hire called in to tell them that he suddenly become allergic to all forms of paint and was now going to pursue a career as a florist. And these are just some examples of the ones who bothered to explain why they were reneging on their commitments; many more simply failed to show up.

The fellow who was at that moment slathering his body in calamine lotion and trying his damnedest not to scratch his spots represented their last hope for outside help, as they had already contacted every other painter within a 50-mile radius of their home.

"You know what this means, don't you?" Arnold asked his wife, his voice filled with resigned despair.

"Yes," she sighed. "We're going to have to paint this place ourselves."

"Damn it!" they cursed together.

*   *   *

In 1970, the mansion was 54 years old and had gone through a surprising number of owners before it landed in the hands of the Hinshaws. Erected on the shore of Wisconsin's West Bay Lake, it had originally been built as a retreat away from the pressures of life in Washington, D.C., by Robert Lamont, who in 1929 earned his highest political position when President Hoover named him Secretary of Commerce.

During the five decades of its existence up to that point, the mansion was never once plagued with the rumors that almost always attach themselves to similar structures around the world. Despite its ever-changing owners, the house was never accused of being haunted or having hosted any kind of diabolical event.

That all changed the year Arnold and Ginger bought the place—changed big time.

From the very first day they moved into the place they knew something wasn't right. While they were still moving in furniture and boxes, they heard the sound of hushed whispering in the halls and caught brief glimpses of vague shapes that could not be mistaken for shadows or tricks of the light. Yet instead of making them rethink living in the mansion, these intriguing paranormal touches seemed to give the mansion a unique character.

"Hey," Arnold joked that day, "if this place really is haunted, we might be able to write a book about it."

But their *laissez-faire* attitude toward the mansion's ghostly quirks quickly faded as the weeks went on and the haunted aspects of the home become more and more disconcertingly real. The sounds of the whispers got louder; the vague flashes of strange shapes grew more frequent. Each night when the Hinshaws sat down for dinner they watched as a full-blown spirit shaped like an old woman floated past them on her way through to the living room's large French doors. They named her Mathilda.

As eerie as all of the paranormal activity was, it could be considered charming as long as it was only in small doses. Then important appliances started acting strangely, working one minute, inexplicably breaking down the next and then working again just as Ginger was ready to call a repairman (who, they would soon learn, wouldn't have arrived anyway).

Then windows started opening and closing on their own, with the doors soon following suit. Once, Arnold was so frustrated by the large window in their bedroom's refusal to stay closed that he hammered a spike into it, ensuring it could never be opened again. Unlike most "securely shut" windows in haunted houses, this one did indeed stay closed for the rest of the family's stay at the house, but not because the spirits of the house couldn't overcome the spike. In fact, it was no match for them at all. Arnold and Ginger were shocked one day to find the spike removed and no hole in either the window's frame or sill—there was no evidence at all that it was ever there to begin with.

Soon all the charm the haunted house might have possessed was gone, and all that remained was the uncomfortable paranoia of not knowing what was going to happen next. Each day presented them with a new incident that qualified as the scariest they had thus far faced. For a time, the worst had to be the morning when Arnold left to go to work and his car engine burst into flames when he started it. From that point on, every car they brought onto the property inevitability experienced unexplainable mechanical difficulties.

But in the end, one incident finally stood out as being by far the most terrifying. And it all began when Arnold and Ginger decided to work on the house by themselves.

*　　　*　　　*

They decided that the first place they would start painting was their bedroom. Unaccustomed to this kind of work they made a mess of it at first but eventually they figured out how to get most of the paint on the wall. They had finished with the room and were about to move on to another when they realized they hadn't painted their bedroom closet. Thinking it would look strange if the interior of the closet was a different color than the walls surrounding it, they opened it up, assuming it would only take a few minutes.

They had lived there for a few months by this time and had used the closet to store their clothes. It was only now, as they began painting it, that they discovered that the shoe cupboard in the back was not attached to the wall, but could be moved out of the way. Assuming that there had to be more wall behind it that needed to be painted, they lifted the cupboard out and discovered that it had been hiding a large hole in the wall.

"What is that?" asked Arnold. "Some sort of secret passageway?"

"No," said Ginger, "I think it's just a hole in the wall."

Deciding that their discovery deserved further investigation, Arnold fetched a flashlight and shined it into the dark crevice. "Uh, honey," he said to his wife as the beam of his flashlight hit on something that looked unpleasantly familiar, "what does this look like to you?"

Ginger took the flashlight from her husband's hand and shined it into the hole. "Arnold," she said quietly, "is that a body wedged inside our wall?"

"I think it is," he answered her.

"A *human* body," she continued, wanting further clarification.

"That would be my guess," he agreed.

By this time the two of them had become so burned-out by the freaky events in their new house that they barely had the energy to react. If they had found a dead body wedged inside their wall at their previous house, their most likely reaction would have been to scream very loudly and call the police, but at Summerwind it was all they could do to loudly curse with annoyance.

A clear sign of how inured they had become to the horrors of their house can be seen in what they immediately chose to do upon making their discovery. Because it was hard to tell—thanks to the plumbing that was in the way—if the human-body shape they had seen really was a human body, they needed someone small enough to crawl inside the hole and get a better look.

"Kids," Ginger called for their children, "come into Mommy and Daddy's room."

All six kids scurried into the room from whichever corner of the house they had been in and looked expectantly at their parents.

Realizing at that moment that it might not be smart to tell them the whole truth about the situation, Ginger came up with a more palatable story to tell them. "Hey guys," she said in that patronizing voice adults adopt when they want to dupe a group of small children, "your dad and I think that the silly-billys who made this house did something crazy! We think they took a bear and put him inside the wall behind our closet. Isn't that silly? The problem is that we can't get a good look to see if they did it or not, so we're going to need one of you to crawl into the space and tell us for sure. Okay?"

Although the children were still young, they had spent enough time in the house to know that there was no bear behind the wall. But, like most kids their ages, they were full of the bravery that comes from not fully being able to contemplate their own mortality.

"I'll do it, Mommy," volunteered Mary, age eight. Ginger handed her daughter the flashlight, and the little girl got on her knees and squeezed into the hole. She stayed in there for about a minute before she crawled back out. "Mommy," she said with total authority, "that isn't a bear. It's a man."

Wanting to share in the fun, all of the other kids insisted on getting a look at the man in the wall.

"We were good parents before we moved into this house, right?" Ginger asked her husband as their young children took turns inspecting the corpse.

"Better than this," Arnold admitted.

"Okay, guys," Ginger lectured her children after they had each had a turn in the hole, "you have to promise me that you won't tell anyone about this."

"Why not?" asked Mary, who had yet to grow out of her "question everything" phase.

"Because it's a game, and the object of the game is to keep a secret forever," Ginger answered her.

"What do we win?"

"What?"

"What do we win if we keep the secret?"

"How about some ice cream?" suggested Arnold.

"Yaaaaaaahhhhhhhhhhh!" all six kids shouted in unison. They were very easy to bribe.

After getting the kids their promised treat, Ginger waited until she and Arnold were alone again before she brought up the subject of the body hidden behind their bedroom closet. "How could it have even gotten there?" Ginger asked her husband.

"The guy must have been murdered while they were building the house," speculated Arnold.

"But wouldn't the men who built the house have seen a body in a wall?"

"I don't know. Maybe they were in on it."

"Should we go to the police?"

"What are they going to do?" asked Arnold. "The guy's been dead for 50 years. Whoever murdered him is probably dead by now too. All calling the cops is going to do is cause an even bigger hole in our closet as they break through our wall and plumbing to get that sucker out of there. Is that a smart thing to do considering our track record with subcontractors? We couldn't get anyone to come over to paint the place; how well are we going to do getting someone to repair broken pipes and drywall?"

"I suppose you're right," said Ginger, even though it didn't sound like she was convinced.

"I say that we keep quiet about this up until the point when he starts stinking up the place. And if he hasn't started yet after all this time, I doubt he's going to start anytime soon."

"I just don't know if I like the idea of sleeping in that room, knowing that he's there."

"We'll switch with one of the kids. They won't care."

"No," said Ginger, "I'm already a candidate for worst mother of the year for sending them in to look at that thing. I'll just deal with it as best I can, I guess."

"Then it's agreed. We don't talk about this with anyone."

"Absolutely."

That night, Arnold nailed a piece of wood over the hole, which they then painted over as if it were part of the wall. From a distance it almost looked like it had been that way forever, and they did their best to forget that the hole was ever there.

*   *   *

Not long after discovering the body in their wall, Arnold started playing his Hammond organ. True, he had played it before they had moved into the mansion, but back then he played it like an organ enthusiast who needed the practice. Now he played it like a demented count in a gothic horror movie.

He often waited until the middle of the night to start playing his dark opuses. They consisted of long compositions that worked hard to avoid the pleasing sound of melody in favor of a droning hum that made his listeners feel like black tar had been poured over their soul.

His songs kept everyone in the house awake, and most nights all six children would join their mother in her bed and huddle together, praying their father would get better.

One night he was working his way through the most discordant of his sinister sonatas when he stopped mid-note and collapsed loudly to the floor. Ginger found him lying there in a state of catatonic shock. She called an ambulance, and after the doctors had diagnosed his collapse as a complete mental breakdown, they sent him to a local psychiatric hospital to get better.

Ginger was now left alone to raise their six kids in the haunted mansion that was their home. Never a strong woman, she soon felt herself succumbing to the same dark forces that had overcome her husband. Each day in Summerwind grew harder and harder to get through. She could not escape the constant whispering of the spirits, nor could she forget the man wedged behind the wall of her bedroom closet. Her nerves frayed past the breaking point, and she decided that she would do anything to have a sense of peace again.

Anything turned out to be swallowing a lot of sleeping pills and chasing them down with a bottle of vodka.

She was found by one of her kids before her deadly cocktail could take effect. An ambulance was called and her stomach was pumped and she lived to see another day—just not in Summerwind. When she became well enough to leave the hospital, she did not go back to her haunted home. She and her children instead went to live with her parents in Granton.

*   *   *

Following the devastation of their mutual breakdowns, Arnold and Ginger divorced. For a time it seemed as though the horror Ginger had gone through at Summerwind was behind her. She met a man named George, married him and moved out of her parents' house. By that point the haunted mansion she had once called home was just an unpleasant memory.

And then her father had a dream.

Raymond Bober had been working as a popcorn vendor during the time his daughter was suffering through the miseries inflicted upon her by the spirits of Summerwind. As he heard her tales of what was happening to her at the mansion, he become more and more fascinated with the world of the paranormal. He started reading every book he could find on the subject and started attending local séances, as well experimenting on his own with an antique Ouija board and learning the art of self-hypnosis.

But it was in the world of dream that Ginger's father got his first clue that he was destined to return to his daughter's former home and search for a treasure he believed would be worth millions. It was while dreaming that he also learned the identity of the ghost that had caused his daughter so much distress.

In his dream he found himself surrounded by hundreds of Native Americans in their traditional tribal garb. From amongst them a white man appeared to Raymond and said, "I brought these people peace, and for that they granted me a tremendous gift. Search for me in the spirit world and help me reclaim it. If you do, then I shall let you reap its incredible rewards." With that the dream ended, leaving Raymond to discover on his own what it had meant and who he should be looking for.

Over the next few days he spent many hours at the spirit board and hypnotizing himself into trances so that he would be more receptive to messages from beyond. Slowly he began to gather the information he was searching for. One night he was given a first name—Jonathan. A few days later a surname arrived to complete the clue—Carver. Thanks to more traditional research, which allowed him to ask the right questions when he communed with the spirits, he was able to piece together the narrative that explained what he had seen in his dream.

Jonathan Carver was an English explorer who, in the late 1700s, traveled through the state that would become Wisconsin. During these travels he found himself caught in the middle of a war being waged by two different nations of Sioux. Thanks to a mixture of bravery and luck he was able to convince the chiefs of the warring nations to meet with him, and together they reached a deal for peace. As thanks for helping to end their long and bloody war, both chiefs signed a deed that turned over to him a large portion of their land—a portion that today would encompass nearly one third of northern Wisconsin.

To protect this precious document, Carver sealed it in a black box, which—in a series of twists and turns Raymond was never fully able to work out—ended up hidden in the foundation of a famous Wisconsin mansion—a place the Ouija board told him was called Summerwind.

Some would call it a coincidence; others would call it fate. Ginger didn't care either way. All she knew was that her father was telling her that he was planning on buying the house that had driven her to attempted suicide and ended her marriage, and she couldn't say or do anything to stop him.

*　　*　　*

Ginger did not want to go back to the house that had wreaked so much ruin upon her life. Nevertheless, when it became clear that her father could not be talked out of his decision to buy the house, search for the lost deed and convert the building into a restaurant, she returned to the mansion with him to explore its mysteries. The thought of what they would find made her stomach churn, especially the thought of a particular skeleton in the closet.

Joining Ginger and her father were her new husband George and her brother Karl. They were both familiar with the stories Ginger had told them about what she had seen happen in the house, but neither of them was ready to fully accept her version of events. Although both she and her ex-husband suffered major breakdowns owing to their time at Summerwind, it was still hard to believe that there was not a more rational explanation for the couple's emotional collapses. They were just as reluctant to buy into Raymond's theories regarding the house, but they both agreed that a restaurant in a beautiful house by the lake could turn out to be a financial success.

The three men toured around the house, with Raymond looking for places where Carver's black box could have been stowed and George and Karl looking for ideas on how it could best be transformed into a restaurant. Ginger stayed alone in the kitchen, which was one of the few spots in the house where nothing strange had ever occurred.

She was prepared to remain there for the entire day, but she changed her mind when she heard her husband come downstairs from the second story and go outside through the front door. Wanting some fresh air, she decided to join him. As she stepped out the front door, she saw that he was getting something from the trunk of their car and asked him what it was.

"This," he answered her by holding up a crowbar.

"What do you need to use that for?" she wondered.

"We were looking around the bedrooms and we saw that in the big one's closet someone nailed a board to wall. We wanted to remove it so we could see what it was covering up."

All of the color drained out of Ginger's face.

"What's wrong?" asked her husband.

"You can't remove that board," she told him. "You have to leave it there! We did that for a reason!"

"What are you talking about?"

"You can't remove that board!" she repeated, her voice reaching the outer edges of hysterical. "You can't!"

George put down the crowbar and rushed over to his wife. He grabbed her by her shoulders and spoke to her in a calm, but authoritative tone. "Ginger," he said, "you have to calm down and tell me what you are talking about."

It took several minutes and them going back inside to the kitchen before Ginger relaxed enough to tell the three men why she didn't want them to remove the board from the closet.

"I promised I'd never tell," she told them. "We should have gone to the police, but Arnold didn't want to and I was so confused."

"Ginger, what happened?" asked her father.

"There's a body behind the closet," she told them. "It is hidden by all sorts of pipes and wooden beams, but it's there."

"But that's impossible," insisted Karl. "We'd be able to smell it if it was there."

"Do you think this house cares if something is impossible or not?" she asked him. "I know what I saw. I know what Arnold saw and I know what my children saw."

"Your children?" asked George.

"We sent them in there to get a better look," she admitted. "We told them it was a bear, but none of them bought it."

All three men just stared at her wordlessly.

"I know," she admitted, "that was not my best moment as a mother. But now you understand why I don't want you to move that board."

The three men looked at each other as they considered her words. After about 10 seconds, they all turned around and ran like a trio of teenagers to the forbidden closet.

Thanks to the crowbar, it took less than 20 seconds to pry loose the board, which revealed a dark hole. A flashlight was found and shone into the hole and revealed…nothing. All they could see was exactly what anyone could reasonably expect to find behind a wall and nothing more.

George went back down to the kitchen and told his wife that they did not find the body she had described.

"What do you mean?" she asked him. "He's right there, behind the wall."

"I'm serious, sweetie," he told her. "There's no one there."

"You're all crazy," she insisted as she started running to the bedroom to prove that what she had seen was still there.

But they weren't crazy—it wasn't there.

"Where did it go?" she asked as she stared into the hole and saw nothing but pipes and wooden beams. "Where did the body go?"

*   *   *

The next weekend Karl returned to the house by himself. He was there to find out how much it was going to cost to rebuild the well out back and to hire an exterminator to take care of the bats housed in the mansion's attic.

His experience at the house the weekend before had done little to convince him that Summerwind was haunted. In fact, by the time he left all he felt he knew for sure was that his sister had probably not completely recovered from her mental breakdown. He could tell by the way she reacted when they opened up that hole in the bedroom closet that she truly believed that she had seen a human body stuffed in there all those months ago. He wondered, as he did some work on the front lawn before the exterminator arrived, what could have happened to her that would have made her mind play such cruel tricks on her.

It didn't take him long to find out.

As he worked outside he felt a few stray drops of water hit him from above. He looked up and saw several serious-looking storm clouds in the sky. He managed to make it inside the house just as those clouds opened up and brought on a powerful thunderstorm that aided immeasurably in giving the old house a spooky aura even Karl couldn't deny.

Remembering that he had left a window open upstairs, Karl ran up to close it before the rain could get in. As he walked down the hallway toward the room the window was in, he heard the sound of someone calling his name.

"Who's that?" he asked aloud. "Is that you, Frank?" he asked, saying the name of the exterminator he had talked to on the phone. No one answered him.

"Must have been a trick of the storm," he decided before he went into the room he had been heading for and closed the open window. Just as he brought the frame down, he heard the same sound again and this time he could tell for sure that it definitely wasn't thunder or a loud wind—it was someone shouting his name.

"What?" he shouted back. "What do you want?"

Again, there was no answer.

Karl was finally getting spooked about being in the big house alone. He walked back downstairs and suddenly flattened himself on to the ground when he heard the sound of two gunshots ring through the house. Karl was very familiar with guns and knew that what he had heard could not be mistaken for the thunder outside. Convinced that a burglar or some other kind of criminal was stalking him inside the house, Karl cautiously got up. He could smell the distinctive odor of gunpowder hovering in the air. He searched the house for the shooter, but it soon became clear that he was completely alone.

But just as he was starting to think he was as crazy as his sister, he discovered two bullet holes in one of the kitchen walls.

They were enough to convince him that it would not be wise for him to spend the night at the mansion. He decided not to wait for the exterminator (who wasn't coming anyway because he had been detained by the storm), and he got in his car and drove back home.

*　　　*　　　*

Just as it had when Ginger and Arnold attempted it, Summerwind managed to resist Raymond's every attempt to renovate it. He had no better luck than his daughter and former son-in-law in getting subcontractors and other laborers to come to the house. For a time he and his wife, Marie, lived in a trailer outside the house. Eventually—after he had spent countless hours chipping away at the building's concrete foundation in search of Carver's black box—he admitted defeat and abandoned the idea of claiming the lost deed as his own and turning the mansion into a successful restaurant.

It turned out to be a wise decision. In 1983, a writer named Will Pooley decided to investigate Raymond's claims about Carver's deed. In his research he discovered that even if Raymond had found such a deed on the property, it wouldn't have been worth the paper it was printed on for multiple reasons. During the period when the was deed supposedly created, the reigning British government had already ruled that individuals could not receive property from Native Americans. Even if there hadn't been such a ruling, the Sioux never owned any property in northern Wisconsin for them to give away to Carver in the first place.

Still, it wasn't a total loss for Raymond. Under the pseudonym Wolffgang Von Bober he published a book called *The Carver Effect* in 1979. In it he described his experiences communing with Carver's spirit and his unsuccessful attempts to renovate Summerwind. He claimed it was Carver's spirit that had been responsible for keeping both him and his daughter from doing any work on the house. He also claimed that the mansion's original owner, Robert Lamont, once fired two shots at Carver's ghost, which was how he explained what had happened to his son Karl when he was alone at Summerwind during the storm.

After Raymond gave up on the house, it quickly fell into disrepair. In 1986, three investors purchased it, also with the intention of turning it into a restaurant, but they too were foiled by a bizarre inability to get anyone to come and work on the place. After two years they were forced to give up on their plans; lightning struck the mansion and it burned to the ground.

The story of Summerwind ends there. The ruins of the old mansion can still be found on the shore of West Bay Lake, along with—some say—the spirits that made it famous.

The Walker House

William Caffee was not someone who was willing to go gently into that good night. If he was going to die, then he was going to do it as loudly and profanely as he could, and he proved it the day they hanged him. It may very well have been the strangest execution that ever took place in the state of Wisconsin, and no one who was there to see it ever forgot it—nor did anyone who was merely told about it afterward. Even now, more than 160 years later, people still remember the day William Caffee was hanged—mostly because William isn't ready to let them forget.

*　　*　　*

William was a violent man, so it was only a matter of time before the law caught up with him and placed a noose around his neck. The crime he was finally convicted of was shooting and killing a man he didn't know in the back. The poor man had bumped into Caffee and had failed to apologize for the accidental contact.

The victim was a stranger in Mineral Point. He possessed no identification of any kind, but since gold was found in his pocket, he was given a proper burial in a spot that was marked with a headstone that simply read, "Here Lies A Stranger Shot Dead By William Caffee on October 25, 1842."

William killed the stranger in front of 20 witnesses, each more than happy to give the testimony that would see him swing. But none of them got the chance because

William happily confessed to his crime and was sentenced to hang just six days after he had committed it.

That first day of November everyone in Mineral Point gathered in front of the Walker-Grundy Inn and waited to see what they expected to be the most entertaining spectacle of the year. William made sure that they weren't disappointed.

Somehow he had convinced his jailers to allow him to ride to his execution in the hearse that had been hired to take his body away when the whole affair was done. Like all condemned men, he had been given the luxury of a last meal of his choice. He chose to have fried steak and potatoes along with two bottles of beer. For reasons no one ever quite figured out, he was allowed to take the two empty beer bottles along with him to his hanging. He used them to beat out an unpleasant, but still recognizable version of a funeral march against his own coffin. Four thousand people had come to Mineral Point to see him die that day, and they all heard him as he serenaded them with a drunken melody that ghoulishly anticipated his own demise.

"Hey, suckers!" Caffee shouted at the onlookers. "I hope you all enjoy the show, because I'm going to give it everything I've got! I'm just dying to entertain ya!"

Caffee's words hit a nerve with some onlookers, who left before they could see him hang, but to everyone else his jokes just made this the most entertaining execution they had ever attended.

The condemned man was brought up to the gallows where a preacher holding a Bible prayed for his sins. "Blah, blah, blah!" Caffee mocked the man. "I know where I'm going, Preacher, and all I can say is that the devil better watch out because a new man is coming to town to raise a little hell!"

To be so glib at one's own hanging was one thing, but outright blasphemy was another. A hushed gasp ran through the crowd as he admitted to one and all that he was looking forward to his eternal damnation.

"String me up already," Caffee said impatiently.

His executors did as he asked and placed the noose around his neck. Back at the jailhouse Caffee had asked to talk to the gallows operator. There he paid the man $20 to ensure that noose's knot was in the right place so that the rope would break his neck and kill him instantly, rather than just cut off his airway and leave him asphyxiating for several long and painful minutes. The hangman was an honest fellow and did right by his word, carefully positioning the knot before he backed away. The trapdoor beneath Caffee's feet opened up.

It turned out that the hangman had done such a good job putting the noose's knot in the right place that the rope didn't merely break Caffee's neck—it took his head right off of his body. The crowd gasped as they witnessed the murderer's decapitation right before their eyes. They gasped and then they started to cheer. This had easily been the most memorable hanging any of them had ever seen.

*　　　*　　　*

People around those parts were still talking about Caffee's death 122 years after it happened. His behavior that day had become something of a local legend, and there were just as many who admired him for the way he refused to be afraid to meet his fate as there were those who despised him for being the murderer that he was.

During those 12 decades, the old inn that had served as the location for Caffee's infamous execution had fallen on hard times. It had closed down in 1957, and since then most of its windows had been broken, its exterior was covered with graffiti and there was no longer any indication that the building had once been one of the swankiest hotels in the entire state.

A group of investors, led by a man named Ted Landon, decided that the hotel's dilapidation wasn't right. They bought the property in 1964 and worked tirelessly for years restoring the building so it could be turned into a beautiful restaurant. Unfortunately, there wasn't much call for this sort of establishment in Mineral Point in 1972. The investors refused to give up and opened another dining room in the building in 1973 and got the tavern going in 1974. But despite all of their efforts, business remained slow, and by 1978 they were ready to sell.

They found a buyer in Dr. David F. Ruf, who promptly hired a fellow named Walker Calvert—a descendent of one of the inn's original builders—to manage the building and cook for the restaurant. It was Calvert who first made the suggestion that the old inn was haunted.

The suspicion started when other employees heard what they thought was their boss having a conversation with another man—a fellow with a low, gravelly voice, the kind that only comes from having drunk too much whiskey and smoked too many cigarettes.

A maid named Georgia once interrupted one of these conversations, but when she did she was shocked to find that Calvert was alone. "Who were you talking to?" she asked him.

Calvert looked over to her and appeared to come out of a daze. "What did you say?" he asked back.

"I asked you who you were talking to," she told him.

He looked at her like she was crazy. "I wasn't talking to anyone," he insisted. "I was all by myself."

"But I swear I heard you talking to someone."

"I think I would know when I was having a conversation with another person," he told her. "Now did you want something?"

She told him that someone wanted to see him in the main dining room.

He thanked her for telling him and then went to see who wanted him.

The dining room was empty when he got there. He was about to turn around and leave when a door panel that was used to allow easy access to the floor's water pipes flung open as if someone had grabbed it.

It was at that moment that he knew something wasn't right about the building. The truth was that he didn't remember talking to anyone earlier, but that was only because he didn't remember anything that had occurred in the half-hour before Georgia came in to talk to him. All he could recall was getting a cup of coffee in the kitchen and then finding himself in another room being spoken to by the maid.

Normally he wouldn't have gotten too concerned about something like this and would have attributed it to fatigue, but now that he had seen something completely unnatural occur in front of his eyes, he knew that there was a frightening explanation for what had happened to him that afternoon.

From that point on things only got worse at the inn.

During the mornings everyone could hear the sound of pots and pans clanging and banging together, even though no one was in the kitchen at that time.

Female staff members and customers complained of an inexplicable, menacing male presence making them uncomfortable. This presence seemed especially fixated with women's hair, and it enjoyed pulling on ponytails and lifting up long strands of hair. A woman's experience of having her hair mysteriously pulled was made even more unnerving by the spirit's heavy breathing, the sound of which had a way of making people feel violated when they heard it.

These strange activities went on for several years before someone finally saw the ghost that was causing all of the trouble. It happened in October 1981 when Calvert saw the ghost sitting alone on the inn's porch. A person might have confused the spirit for a normal man, were it not for the fact that it didn't have a head on its shoulders.

Although Caffee had long been suspected of being the cause of all of the trouble and mischief that had occurred at the inn, this confirmed it. Of all the people who died in or around the inn in its history, he was the only one who lost his head in the process.

*   *   *

The ghost of William Caffee remains at the Walker House to this very day. His spirit is as feisty as ever, pulling hair and breathing hard wherever he's found. Despite his threat to terrorize the devil in hell, his spirit remains at the site where his twisted, angry life came to an end. One can only assume that the devil prefers it that way.

The Final Curtain

The doctor had made it clear to her family that Mary Tubey had—at most—only a day or two left before the disease he still could not name would end her life. Among those gathered at her Milwaukee home was her step-brother, Dan Connell, who despaired at the thought of a world without one of the kindest and most gentle people he had ever been lucky enough to know. He stayed at the house until he could no longer keep his eyes open, but when he returned to his own home he could not sleep knowing that Mary might—at that very moment—be breathing her last breath.

When he returned to Mary's house the next morning she was still alive, but only for a matter of minutes. After suffering so much pain, Mary Tubey died in the early morning hours of September 21, 1878, and Dan was there, among others, to witness her last moment on this Earth—or so he thought.

Worn out from a lack of sleep and engulfed by grief, he returned home and told his wife, Susan, that his step-sister was dead. She tried to ease his mind by preparing him a nice lunch, but he had no appetite and had little energy to do anything but sit in the front room and stare out the large picture window. He tried to take solace in all of the life he saw pass by in front of him, but there was no comfort to be found—he could think only of Mary and the horrible truth that he would never hear her beautiful laugh again.

Dan was not a man who believed in tears. Not once since he was a small child had he let any roll down his cheeks, but at that moment he was helpless to stop them.

He let them fall, but not before he turned away from the picture window so that no one outside could see him in his moment of weakness. His eyes now faced the doorway to his and Susan's bedroom. The door was open and sunshine lit up the room.

He turned his gaze to that room's window, which was decorated by curtains that Mary had sewn as a present for his and Susan's last wedding anniversary. He didn't know enough about fabric to tell what the curtains were made of, but he had always found them to be quite charming, and he found himself studying them in a way that distracted him from his tears.

Susan was busy dealing with her grief her own way—working on a quilt she intended to dedicate to Mary's memory—when she was startled by the sound of her husband shouting from their bedroom. "Susan!" he cried. "It's a miracle! Susan, come here! You have to come!"

When she reached the bedroom she found her husband on his knees, as if he no longer had the strength to stand. "What is it, Dan?" she asked him.

"Can't you see it?" asked her husband.

"See what?"

"There!" He pointed to the curtain that decorated the bedroom's window.

Susan's eyes focused to where Dan was pointing, and she saw what had gotten him so excited. It was Mary's face—as clear as day.

Susan fainted dead away.

*   *   *

Within hours, news of the apparition in the curtain had spread throughout the entire neighborhood. The Connells, believing this blessing was meant to be shared, allowed everyone who arrived at their doorstep to come in and see it for themselves. Many gasped when they saw it, while some claimed—when they were out of the house and in no danger of offending their hosts—that they had seen nothing at all. But by dinnertime the crowd of curious folks had grown so large that the Connells could no longer accommodate them. They locked their doors and told everyone to come back tomorrow.

The next day the crowds were even larger than before, but at least this time the air was warmer than it had been, and the constantly open door failed to cool the house. But the reactions were just as polarized as they had been the day before, with many people certain that the face was there and a smaller percentage equally certain that they were serving witness to a massive case of group psychosis. The vision lasted until dusk, when both Dan and Susan agreed that Mary's face had faded away from sight.

Still there were many people outside who had not gotten their chance to inspect the curtain for themselves, and they refused to leave just because the Connells insisted that the face was no longer there. As they filed past the now completely normal curtain, most agreed that there was nothing to see, but some people insisted the face was still there.

Was it ever really there? Were the Connells really visited by the presence of Mary Tubey? Or was what they saw merely the product of their grief, given credence by the desire of others to believe in the possibility of miracles? We'll never know the answer to these questions, but one thing we can say for certain is that not a single day went by that Dan and Susan didn't give that curtain good look to see if Mary had returned.

The End

Ghostly Glossary

ANGELS: Derived from the Greek word *angelos* ("messenger"), angels are the celestial messengers and guardians of a deity; though often associated with Christianity, angels are common to many religions. They are immaterial beings, sexless creatures of pure consciousness that possessed a knowledge no mortal could ever even hope to comprehend.

CLAIRAUDIENT: An individual with the ability to perceive sound or words beyond the range of hearing. These sounds can come from outside sources such as spirits or other entities. Clairaudience is said to be a form of channeling messages through audible thought patterns.

COLD SPOTS: Commonly associated with haunted sites, a cold spot is said to result from a ghost absorbing the necessary energy to materialize from its surroundings. They are usually quite localized and are 10 or more degrees cooler than the surrounding area.

DEMON: In Christian theology, demons are the instruments of evil, the fallen angels cast out of heaven with Lucifer. They exist for no other purpose but to torment and torture the living through abuse, assault and possession. However, in other cultures, demons are not nearly so malicious. To the Greeks, daimons (translated, the word means "divine power") served as intermediaries between mortals and the gods of Mount Olympus.

ECTOPLASM: A term popularized in the film Ghostbusters, ectoplasm is said to be a white, sticky, goo-like substance with a smell resembling ozone. It is, hypothetically, a dense bio-energy used by spirits to materialize as ghosts. Its existence has never been proven.

EMF: An electromagnetic field, or EMF, is a region where magnetism created by electrically charged objects can be detected. Many paranormal researchers equate an EMF with paranormal activity, believing that ghosts generate high levels of electromagnetic energy through their activities.

ESP: Extrasensory Perception, or ESP, describes the ability to perceive and receive information without the use of any of the usual five senses: sight, touch, smell, hearing and taste. Not surprisingly, ESP is often referred to as the sixth sense.

EVP: Electronic Voice Phenomena, or EVP, is a process through which the voices of the dead are captured on an audiocassette. How the process works is a bit of a mystery, but it usually involves placing a tape recorder at a haunted site. When played back, the voices of the dead should be clear on the recording and should not be confused with background noise or static.

EXORCISM: An exorcism is the purging of a person, place or thing that has been possessed by a demon or other unnatural force. It is normally carried out under the close supervision of a religious official, thoroughly trained and capable.

GEIGER COUNTER: An instrument that detects and measures radioactivity, or the spontaneous emission of energy from certain elements. This device searches for fluctuations in Alpha, Beta, Gamma and X-ray radiation, which point to a disturbance in spirit energy.

GHOST: Derived from the German word *geist* and the Dutch word *geest*, a ghost is the physical manifestation of an individual's disembodied spirit. It may appear as a figure, but a ghost can also manifest itself through smells, sounds and other sensations. At the heart of any belief concerning ghosts is the idea of a separation between the physical body and the metaphysical soul. The body perishes, though the soul does not.

MATERIALIZATION: The process through which seemingly solid objects or individuals appear out of thin air. It was a popular and well-documented phenomenon during the earliest years of Spiritualism, when mediums commonly caused objects like coins and cups to materialize.

ORBS: Though they may vary in shape, color and size, orbs are most commonly round in shape and whitish gray in color and are usually, though not always, found in photographs taken during a haunting or at a haunted site. They are believed to represent the spirit of the dead. Because dust, moisture and lens flare can easily be confused with orbs, some critics have argued that orbs may not be enough proof to legitimize a haunting.

OUIJA BOARD: An instrument that allegedly can be used to contact or channel spirits of the deceased. It is usually a wooden or cardboard device inscribed with the alphabet, the words "yes" and "no" and the numbers 0 to 9. There is usually a slideable apparatus on rotating castors or wheels with a pointer. The operators of the board place their fingers lightly on the slideable device and wait for it to move.

PARANORMAL: Any event that cannot be explained or defined through accepted scientific knowledge is said to be beyond what is normal. It is, therefore, paranormal.

POLTERGEIST: A combination of two German words, *poltern* (to knock) and *geist* (spirit), a poltergeist is characterized by its bizarre and mischievous behavior. Activities of a poltergeist include, but are not limited to, the moving of furniture, the throwing of objects and the rapping and knocking of walls. A poltergeist may also be responsible for terrible odors and cries. Typically, the activities of a poltergeist appear unfocused, pointless and completely random.

POSSESSION: A condition in which all of an individual's faculties fall under the control of an external force, such as a demon or deity. An individual possessed by a demon may alter his or her voice, even his or her appearance, and be fearful of religious symbols.

REVENANT: From the French *revenir* (to return), a revenant is a ghost that appears shortly after its physical death. Usually, it will only appear a few times, perhaps even just once, before disappearing from the earth forever.

SPIRITUALISM: A movement that originated in the United States in 1848, Spiritualism is a religion whose beliefs are centered upon the idea that communication with the dead is altogether possible. By the late 19th century, spiritualism had become popular throughout the United States. Its popularity ebbed in the early 20th century as many of the religion's earliest mediums were exposed as frauds, but rose again after World War I. It is still popular today.

THERMOGRAPH: A self-recording thermometer that traces temperature variations over time.

TRANCE: A trance is essentially an altered state of consciousness in which the individual, though not asleep, is barely aware of his or her immediate environment. There is some speculation that during a trance, the body enters a state that hovers somewhere between life and death, which frees the mind to explore a higher realm and gain spiritual insight.

A.S. Mott

Author A.S. Mott has a penchant for combining a fascination with the supernatural with an offbeat sense of humor, a talent that has served him well in writing to date ten popular volumes of ghost stories. Mott says that, as a child, he didn't care to play outside and preferred instead the relatively dark confines of his parents' basement. In the gloom, he fed his fears and his fancies with a steady diet of scary movies and the most frightening books he could find. It is hardly surprising, therefore, that Mott today is an accomplished writer on the subject of the paranormal and a trivia expert of the first order when it comes to horror films.

LONE
PINE

Lone Pine Publishing International

ENJOY MORE FASCINATING ACCOUNTS OF AMERICA'S PARANORMAL FOLKLORE.

Ghost Stories of Minnesota *by Gina Teel*

Read about the spirit of a young mother still tending to her infant son on the third floor of the historic Warden's House in Stillwater; the ill-tempered ghost of a gangster caught on film trying to muscle in on a wedding at the Landmark Center in St. Paul; and Art, a coverall-clad handyman ghost haunting the Rochester Repository Theater.

$10.95USD/$14.95CDN • ISBN10: 1-894877-07-1 • ISBN13: 978-1-894877-07-7 • 5.25" x 8.25" • 232 pages

Ghost Stories of Michigan *by Dan Asfar*

These tales of fright-filled folklore span the length and breadth of the Great Lakes State. Stories include those of a phantom lighthouse keeper who continues to help, a ghostly light outside the town of Paulding, and a helpful apparition of an actress in Calumet.

$10.95USD/$14.95CDN • ISBN10: 1-894877-05-5 • ISBN13: 978-1-894877-05-3 • 5.25" x 8.25" • 224 pages

Ghost Stories of Ohio *by Edrick Thay*

Ohio's paranormal legacy contains many strange tales: the spirit of a jilted Egypt Pike man spends his afterlife terrifying contented lovers; the ghosts of many victims of a horrific train wreck return search for answers; a mysterious creature baffles terrified witnesses on the Ohio–West Virginia border;…and more.

$11.95USD/$14.95CDN • ISBN10: 1-894877-09-8 • ISBN13: 978-1-894877-09-1 • 5.25" x 8.25" • 232 pages

Ghost Stories of Texas *by Jo-Anne Christensen*

Along with its Wild West spirit, geographical diversity, dramatic history and sheer size, Texas contains a wealth of spooky stories of the supernatural. Enjoy tales from the Alamo, Big Bend National Park, Dallas, Fort Worth, Laredo, Galveston, Corpus Christi and more.

$11.95usd/$14.95cdn • ISBN10: 1-55105-330-6 • ISBN13: 978-1-55105-330-1 • 5.25" x 8.25" • 232 pages

Ghost Stories of Illinois *by Jo-Anne Christensen*

For anyone interested in the paranormal, Ghost Stories of Illinois is sure to prove a chilling and unforgettable treat. Enjoy tales of ghostly visitations—among them spirits from the Great Chicago Fire, the curse of the St. Valentine's Day Massacre, a spectral steamboat on Fulton County's Spoon River and the wandering ghost of Abe Lincoln.

$11.95usd/$14.95cdn • ISBN10: 1-55105-239-3 • ISBN13: 978-1-55105-239-7 • 5.25" x 8.25" • 240 pages

Ghost Stories of Indiana *by Edrick Thay*

Indiana, Crossroads of America, is a place where spirits and ghosts intermingle with the lives of ordinary Hoosiers. Shrunken heads, a peculiar hidden altar and chilling screams split the night in an Indiana University residence. The mischievous ghost of football hero George Gipp spooks students at the University of Notre Dame. The spirit of aviatrix Amelia Earhart returns to spend time at Purdue University. These and many other stories await you in Ghost Stories of Indiana.

$11.95usd/$14.95cdn • ISBN10: 1-894877-06-3 • ISBN13: 978-1-894877-06-0 • 5.25" x 8.25" • 240 pages

**These and many more LPPI books are available
from your local bookseller or by ordering direct.
U.S. readers call 1-800-518-3541. In Canada, call 1-800-661-9017.**